P9-AGI-710

**"HAUNTING . . .
DELIGHTFUL . . .
A MAGICAL FABLE"**
The New York Times

One memorable day, while scanning the western coast of Ireland for British Naval Intelligence during World War II, Ronald Lockley caught a glimpse of a dark-haired girl swimming in a school of seals. The memory lingered on. Although Lockley never saw the girl again, he did return to uncover her legend, the legend of the seal-woman of Kilcalla. From it he has woven this rare and tragic tale of love between a perfectly natural woman and a young naval officer.

"Beautiful, unusual, moving, this has the same dream-like quality of Hudson's GREEN MANSIONS."
School Library Journal

Ronald Lockley, British naturalist and writer, is the author of THE PRIVATE LIFE OF THE RABBIT, the sourcebook for Richard Adams' WATERSHIP DOWN.

Other Avon Books by
Ronald Lockley

THE PRIVATE LIFE OF THE RABBIT   25957 $5.95

Seal-Woman
Ronald Lockley

◆ AVON
PUBLISHERS OF BARD, CAMELOT AND DISCUS BOOKS

Cover illustration inspired by *The Mermaid* by Howard Pyle.

AVON BOOKS
A division of
The Hearst Corporation
959 Eighth Avenue
New York, New York 10019

Copyright © 1975 by Ronald Lockley
Published by arrangement with Rex Collings, Ltd.
Library of Congress Catalog Card Number: 77-80561
ISBN: 0-380-00797-5

All rights reserved, which includes the right
to reproduce this book or portions thereof in
any form whatsoever. For information address
Avon Books.

First Avon Printing, August, 1977

AVON TRADEMARK REG. U.S. PAT. OFF. AND IN
OTHER COUNTRIES, MARCA REGISTRADA,
HECHO EN U.S.A.

Printed in Canada

The tree-wind is blind with the shade of the trees,
The sea-wind is dumb with the roar of the seas.

—from a legend of south-western Ireland

Chapter One

Now that the danger is over and the nature of our mission is forgotten and the surveys and observations we made pigeonholed in some dusty niche at Whitehall I suppose I am at liberty to explain how it was that I encountered the seal-woman of Kilcalla, as, but for that mission, this strange story could never have been told.

The main purpose in exploring the coast of Eire in a small boat was to ferret out possible landing places which the enemy might be using on the wilder and more inhospitable shores. It was a time when enemy submarines were known to have visited such places at night. As Gerald and I both loved small boats the mission was for us in the nature of a delightful holiday and one which we would have undertaken with the greatest ardor even in peace-time. To be ordered by the Naval Intelligence Division of the Admiralty to leave our then rather humdrum Channel patrol duties, and to be commanded to set forth on such an expedition, had filled us with joy. Not only that, but the survey took place in the height of summer, so that on some of the loveliest days from June to August, our work for the day over, we would anchor at ease, watching the sea-birds and seals, swimming and fishing near them ourselves, in some wild bay or creek, or under the lee of some uninhabited island. When the sun set in the boundless western ocean, one of us would sleep, while the other kept watch upon the star-lit water.

It was difficult to imagine that these magnificent cliffs, tumbled rocks and wild empty sandhills would ever experience a war more terrible than that waged by the west wind. It was a thousand years since the last invasion, when the Vikings had landed in Western Ireland, and brought their blond looks and blue eyes to influence the destiny of the pagan and Christian peoples of Iberian and Goidelic origin.

We were not far from the end of our mission when we drew in to the most rugged sweep of all that wild south-western coast, the name of which—on the chart there is no name—we did not at first discover. Gerald, who is an Irishman from Donegal, called it Kilcalla, saying the name sweetly in his Irish brogue, from the fact that the hill region behind the coast had this title on our land map. Let me add only this: that it lies somewhere on that little-known stretch of coast which runs from Valentia Island south to Cape Clear.

As you sail southwards you will see an immense red cliff, and not far beyond and above are the heath-covered mountains. From three miles at sea it seems impossible that a boat could land anywhere on this great walled-in coast.

Then as you sail nearer the details emerge; first the emerald slope beyond the solid phalanx of rocks forming the near headland. Once you have negotiated the tide-race at this cape you enter a wide bay beneath a thousand-foot cliff, granite, with green ledges, while to the south a confusion of brown-gray rock masses, huge, menhir-like, as if the pagan gods had thrown down their mighty stone phalli and altars there, terminates the landward view. Across this bight it must be nearly two miles. This fine empty bay has a steep beach of broad flat pebbles. From high water mark to the edge of the escarpment seven hundred feet above, the central part is softened with the greens and yellows of gorse and flowering maritime plants. The strand faces west and in gales receives the full strength of the Atlantic swell. Only on such a day as this was it possible to land in a small boat.

The wind was north-east, so that as we skirted the shore and came under the shelter of the northerly cape the breeze failed us. Gerald dropped our sail, as we glided to the beach. Whenever we could we avoided using the engine—silence was useful if we were to sur-

8

prise the enemy hiding behind some headland or island; and besides we were both ardent sailing men.

The guttural cries of sea-birds came to us, softened by the lapping of our bow-wave, as they flew between cliff and water. Within easy gunshot were a dozen seals whose brown heads were turned toward us as if in wonder at this intrusion. They were extraordinarily tame. Evidently this sanctuary was little visited by hostile fishermen.

Great caves yawned before us under the first headland. We heard the snorting of more seals far up in the dark recesses.

"A God-forsaken lonely place," said Gerald, but my own heart was stirred beyond comment just then; and even Gerald qualified his remark with a muttered ". . . in winter. Calm enough today, I should think even the Jerries would funk landing here . . . too exposed."

It seemed to me that this forgotten shore, filled with the beauty of untouched nature and the clean sea, and cut off from human contact by the high rampart of the cliffs, was what I had always longed to find. This was the inviolate retreat dreamed of in boyhood, but now as a man engaged in a ruthless war I sensed an indefinable sadness in its discovery.

The sun was close upon the edge of the ocean. The high cliff had assumed a roseate tinge. Blacker shadows were playing in the fissures of the rocks, drawing velvet curtains across the entrances to the caves, as we lowered the dinghy.

"We may as well anchor here; it's calm enough just for one night."

As a boy I had often wondered where gulls slept, and had sometimes, when on holidays, searched for them along the mainland shore—only to watch them at sunset drifting far out over the sea. No doubt, I had thought, they were seeking some remote island or uninhabited strand where man could not surprise them by night. This lonely shore was lined with a great array of gulls gathered to roost. It was a sanctuary for every sort of wild creature. Nor were they much disturbed by our simple preparations to join them.

9

We moored the boat, and while Gerald put up the tent, I took a sack and began climbing the grassy slope in search of dead twigs for our fire. We had seen a white goat far up on the escarpment, and I found narrow pitted animal tracks as I moved upwards. This was not surprising; on many remote cliffs of the Irish coast wild goats can be found, and Gerald's gun had now and then brought down a tender kid for the pot.

By the time I had got half-way up the bush-filled scree I was out of breath. I threw myself down on a grassy platform beside a rivulet of clear water, to drink thirstily.

The sun was vanishing with a green flash in the west. There was a fine weather look in the purple mist where the edges of the darkening sea touched the massive horns of the bay.

For a moment I forgot my errand of collecting sticks—and looking for signs of enemy landing (surely there could be none here?)—in the ease of resting on my green couch and studying the landscape. We had had a long day at sea. I was pleasantly tired. When the distant chattering of the gulls ceased on the beach below as they settled to their early rest, I closed my eyes in a half-sleep.

Mingled with the last notes of the gulls I heard a sweet sound, mistaking it at first for the song of the sea on the pebbles. Gerald and I are both fond of music—and for a moment I was seized by an ecstasy or swoon of delight at the trembling notes. Soon I could fix the true direction of a treble voice singing afar off, mingling with the other sounds of nature—the trickling of the rill beside me, the faint wash of a wave, the warning clack of a blackbird in the thicket near me, and now and then a distinct bleating note.

I struggled to my feet, remembering the white goat. Looking up toward where I had last seen the animal, I was amazed to see the figure of a young woman—she was scarcely more than an adolescent girl—high up on the cliff. Her blue dress was in sharp contrast with the pure white of three or four goats which were following close around her. I had one glimpse of her heels—they were bare.

She disappeared behind a shoulder of rock, and I saw her no more. I resumed my stick-collecting.

That night Gerald and I warmed ourselves against the cool sea air by our supper fire on the flat pebbles. Gerald asked me if I had spoken to the goat-herdess. He had first noticed her singing in the thickets close to the shore. Then she had come down in full view of the beach, and stared at him.

She seemed surprised to discover a boat, and a man . . .

"No," he said in answer to my query, "she did not speak to me. In fact she kept well away when I called out a greeting. As far as I could see she was just a young girl, hardly full grown. Shy, I expect. Suspicious of a rough character like me, no doubt! Anyway she stopped singing when she saw me. Then she called to the goats and went straight up the cliffs like a goat herself, and vanished in the vegetation. I thought you might have run into her."

I was intrigued by the whole affair, because Gerald had caught the gist of the song she had been singing. His attentive ear was ever ready to record the folk songs and tales of his native Irish people, for he had been reared in the Erse language.

We talked while the heavens filled with stars. There was not a cloud between the land and the horizon. With our pipes going around the fire he brought out his notebook, in which he had scribbled the words of the goat-girl's song in its original Irish; and with his keen sense of musical notation he had marked its cadences. He even tried to sing it to me—having warmed himself with some Irish poteen (so easily obtained on that coast). As I could not then understand more than a few words of Erse I could only enjoy his good bass voice.

Later he translated it into English, very roughly, saying that the ballad lost much of its true feeling and rhythm in the process:

11

Song of my heart, O sea, thou art singing,
Down there in the white strand thou are beating;
Thy music is under my head in the heather,
Thy music is in my ear when of thee I am dreaming;
For I have given my heart to the sea
   and the folk of the sea.

In the morning I woke to find the great cliff in shadow above us. High in the sky the narrowed wings of the gulls were a translucent pattern against the sun's light: as if hung on an invisible thread under the eggshell blue of the morning firmament each gull held the air unmoving, head pointed inland toward the mountains. Thus I knew that a strong east wind was blowing from the sun, while yet the land gave us perfect shelter. As if in answer to my thought a little white cloud darted from the cliff seawards, and as my eyes sleepily followed it I saw that the open ocean was white-capped with the dawn wind.

Then I thought of the goat-girl, and of her song, and remembered that I had just had a vivid dream of walking in the woods with her, of talking with a beautiful young woman . . . she was asking me something, but I could not remember what, only it seemed important to her, while I—in this dream—was absorbed with gazing on her exciting form. It was almost an erotic dream, such as young men experience from time to time . . .

Over our simple breakfast Gerald and I made our usual plans for the day. He regretted he had not been bolder and spoken to the goat-girl, detained her until he had got more of that song from her. There was more than one verse, but he had been able to memorize only a few lines—he thought it was the refrain he had heard; he was sure she had repeated some lines at least twice in his hearing. Irish ballads invariably had a refrain or chorus, to emphasize and prolong the singer's story.

We agreed we could not stop long here; we were due that evening at the next port, where a trawler was to meet us for refueling and sealed orders. But we had been given some license of a day or so extra if necessary. A slight swell was coming to the shore, washed back from the fresh land wind at sea. I had better complete my reconnaissance for signs of enemy penetration quickly (you could never be sure, but we agreed we were unlikely to find anything suspicious in such a wild inaccessible spot for landing) with a quick check-up of the road approaches to this beach by which supplies might be slipped secretly to enemy vessels.

Leaving Gerald to complete the usual mapping of possible dinghy landing sites, I attacked the cliff slope eagerly. There was no clear path. I forced one through thickets of sloe, privet, elder and whitehorn. The yellow, white and red trumpets of the honeysuckle decorated profusely this curtain of vegetation; its heavy sweet scent was beginning to awaken, although the land was yet in cold shadow. The luxuriant maritime variety of red campion at my feet was soaked with dew. Little goat paths zigzagged confusedly in and out, small help to my ascent. I blundered upwards, disturbing the ring-doves and small birds which seem to throng in this sanctuary.

The great escarpment had many surprises and delights. A broad green shelf of closely nibbled turf unexpectedly opened before me; it had been grazed by the goats. A wall of iron-gray slate rock rose sheer from this grassy dais, and at first there seemed no way out. The dusky green fronds of royal fern offered too precarious a step-ladder in the upper fissures.

Then I noticed a low avenue where the grass ledge and the black cliff narrowed to a verdurous point. A tunnel of the summer-green leaves of thorn and ash passed through a mossy stairway upwards, wet from a multitude of tiny springs. But soon the path was more open, though steeper and marked with rough steps, passing by a break in the cliff, up and up.

Had I not seen human footprints? Not the clumsy boot-shod prints of man, but marks of neat small toes lay in the damp places. Some were partly obliterated by the hoof-marks of goats, but fresh prints showed that the girl or young woman had used this path, probably when I had seen her yesterday.

Now I must be five hundred feet high. I looked down and saw Gerald far below, rowing out in the dinghy, a thumbnail on the blue rim of ocean. At sea the offshore wind was raising a translucent eddy or whirlwind of spray which swept toward and blurred the western horizon. Yet up here in the shelter of the cliff there was scarcely a breath of wind. I must hurry; soon Gerald would be fussing about tides and time.

Up and up. My breath came in great gasps. I was stepping over a steep slippery scree of slate slabs, possibly the outfall of some long-abandoned quarry. There was little vegetation to lay hold on here—yellow and gold and gray lichens, and now and then an uncompromising gorse bush.

At last—seven hundred feet—I reached the edge of the cliff and felt the warm sun and cool east wind on my wet brow.

I was standing on a grassy ridge, two hundred yards wide, covered with short wind-bitten vegetation. My botanizing eye noted the rare large-petaled centaury sprinkled over a turf thick with white rock-rose, yellow hawkweed and gold-centered oxeye daisies, slowly unfolding to the morning sun.

Beyond this carpet of wild flowers a barrier of high thorn trees guarded the edge of a forest which filled the whole of the lower slopes of the nearest mountains. A wild and beautiful setting, and again my heart was uplifted. I wanted to plunge into the trees and explore every corner of this wilderness.

One day I would come back here and do so—when this damnable war was over. But meanwhile I had no moments to spare if I would complete my reconnaissance.

Little paths criss-crossed the short turf in all directions, some more worn than others. Judging by the pellets marking this blossomy meadow, here was the playground of the wild creatures of both cliff and forest.

Still breathless, I rested, alert, sprawling in the cool dew. I started inland. Rabbits hopped and grazed, magpies were squabbling over something lying in the grass near the edge of the wood, a great flight of

14

ravens was twisting and turning in the wind above the trees as they sailed on leisurely, wings seawards, evidently coming from some sheltered roosting place inland.

Ah, what was that? I raised myself to stare at a tawny animal running along the edge of the wood. Soon more appeared—five in all, and I could see that they were dappled. Now they were leaping into the open, their graceful forms catching the sunlight.

Undoubtedly it was a fallow deer family group, a good-sized male with well-branched horns, and two does, each with her fawn.

Their behavior puzzled me. Something had alarmed them; but they had not seen me yet, as I crouched in the grass. They kept glancing toward the woods, then bounding in my direction, then pausing to look back again.

And at last I saw what was disturbing them. It was my goat-herdess!

She had emerged from the wood, followed by five or six white goats which at first made her dress appear dingy until, as she came out into the morning sunlight, I saw it was a faded blue—its ragged edges barely reached her knees. Her face was very brown at that distance, and now her hair, appearing in two long black pigtails thrown forward over her breast, made her seem a mere child.

Absorbed in watching this beautiful group, at first I did not notice that the deer were moving toward the girl and her goats. Why, how tame they were, these wild animals, how ridiculously tame!

But they were not completely fearless, after all. Led by the buck they came daintily forward until they were only a few paces from the goats, one of which stepped forward to touch the nose of the buck. Then suddenly, sniffing nervously, the deer ran off about twenty yards. They came forward again when the girl put out one hand toward them coaxingly; only to bound back again, nosing the air repeatedly.

The girl had turned her head back toward the woods. The goats began to wander and graze. I heard her call several times toward the trees a name of some sort, but could only catch the lilting note, and I knew beyond doubt now that this was the voice I had heard yesterday, singing that strange song in Irish, about the sea and the music of the sea.

Should I stand up and walk toward her? The impulse was strong. But the observer in me bade me lie in the slight fold of the ground, and wait and see what might be going on. There was someone else in the wood.

The second person proved to be a man, and even as he emerged from the trees I saw that he was carrying a gun at his shoulder, and wearing some kind of uniform.

His appearance was too much for the deer. They darted off, swinging in a wide circle until they vanished along the perimeter of the woods.

The man and girl seemed to be in conference; their voices were too far away for me to hear. The girl was gesticulating. They seemed to come to a decision, for the girl nodded emphatically, and began running, bounding like a deer as she followed the edge of the woods, at a right angle to my position. Again I saw that her feet were bare. The goats, evidently alarmed at the departure of their mistress, suddenly bleated, and in a troop began cantering after her. But she only increased her pace, easily outdistancing them; and soon they slowed theirs, pausing to nibble a mouthful here and there, but reluctant to lose sight of her. They continued to bleat protestingly after she had vanished.

I lay concealed for a while, watching the man. He had swung his gun to the ready position, but as soon as the girl disappeared he began striding forward toward the cliffs. As this was likely to bring him close past me, I knew it would be useless to remain concealed any longer, even had I wanted to.

I stood up. He saw me immediately and altered course. He was young, though tall and strongly built, wearing the jacket of the Irish coastguard. His right hand had gone to the barrel of his rifle.

He stopped within ten paces and called out a "good morning" in Irish. His expression was stern yet

16

pleasant, his skin brown and clear, his eyes blue and hair blond—not at all the usual type for a south-western Irishman.

"Good morning," I replied in English, and said quickly that I supposed he wanted to know my business. I opened my wallet and held out the letter which gave our names and the identification letters of our boat, and asked coastguards to give us every help in their power. (The "neutral" Eire authorities had consented to render this assistance to the Royal Navy—unofficially, of course.)

His wary look relaxed as he read the letter, while we stood at arm's length. Then he looked up, saying:

"Letters VW. Yes, sir, I think I remember that on my instructions."

"You should have had a confidential warning of our presence about this time in this district."

He drew out his notebook and searched through it. Yes, I was fully in order—he spoke with respect now—and he hoped I was having a successful passage. Could he help? Any signs of secret enemy landings farther along the coast? None here at all—too wild a spot, but up the coast he had heard that in the shelter of Va-lentia Island . . . He spoke English with the soft sibilant voice of the people of County Kerry.

He sat down in the shelter of a rock and talked for a while of the war; and then I asked the question which was burning on my lips:

"Who was that girl with the goats?"

For a moment he hesitated, as if reluctant to answer. His face was redder when at last he said:

"Sure, sir, she's only my sister Shian. A wild little divil yet, if ever there was one. It was she who told me of a boat in the bay, when I came home after midnight from town. It was too late to do anything in the darkness, so I came out first thing this morning."

It was a slow business, getting the information I wanted. But the more he said, the more unusual was his tale. It appeared that he and his sister lived with their grandparents in the nearby farm. Their parents had died young—he could not remember them. He had been away in a boarding school but Shian had run wild in this wildest of wild places, where there were still deer, marten, otter, badger and fox in plenty, and seals in number along the shore. He spoke, with a surge of pride now, of the great herd of wild cattle, and was surprised I knew nothing about them. Why, the white cattle of Kilcalla were famous in Ireland, were said to be the oldest wild white cattle in Europe! They lived free in the woods and park of the family estate here. Great animals with huge horns and black-tipped ears—they were for beef, you couldn't milk them. That's why they kept goats for milk. Once or twice a year the white cattle were rounded up, for branding and to pick out the young steers and calves for sale.

With deft questions I coaxed Brendan O'Malley to talk about his life in this remote place. It had become a rough and lonely existence, he confessed. Since the war started there were no servants left, only the bailiff. Grandfather O'Malley was a proud son of a gun, used to the autocratic way of life, natural enough in one of the last of the princes of Eire. Why, indeed, at his age should he bend the knee to inquisitive government officials and the new-fangled compulsory orders of Irish Ministries of this and that? Anyway you couldn't reason with him or with her. The old pair had lived so long to themselves that it was hopeless to get them to agree to any change, or admit any authority but their own. As to the estate, well, it was no longer a neat establishment full of paid helpers and retainers as of old. It had become a cattle ranch with scarcely a whole gate or fence left, or cottage intact upon it.

Brendan continued to avoid my further questions about his sister. And time was running out—I would have to tear myself away, back to the boat. Gerald would be anxious, for the wind had not gone down. It whistled wildly over the rock behind which we sheltered. But the story Brendan had begun to unfold was so strange that had it not been for the anxiety and honesty in his eyes and voice I might have thought it pure Irish blarney.

What was this absurd tale about the last reigning

princes of Ireland? Again I pressed him to talk, confessing my genuine interest in the lineage of the ancient Irish stock. He was naïvely surprised that I was so ignorant of the House of Kilcalla.

Gradually he spoke more easily, naturally, as we sat together in the morning sunshine. He was, he said, but with a modest shrug of the shoulders, descended from the "line royal" of Irish kings and princes—the O'Malleys traced their descent directly from the Vikings of Scandinavia who had first landed on the Kilcalla Strand. They had founded a kingdom here by conquest, a settlement of tall blue-eyed men who had exacted toll and tribute from the small dark Irish natives. Later they had married the high-born women of the neighboring estates of ruling Irish Chieftains descended from the earlier settlers, the tribes of the Goidelic Celts. Their lands, thus joined, once covered half the western shores and mountains. Now they were shrunk to the thousand acres or so of Kilcalla. He and Shian and their grandparents were the only ones left of their family, which in the present century seemed under a cloud, or spell of ill luck. Grandfather was over eighty, deaf and almost helpless. The management of the estate was in the hands of a loyal but hopelessly inefficient—because he was so old—bailiff . . .

Well, he—Brendan—didn't really care any more about Kilcalla. He was quite sick of the place, decaying and gone to seed more and more each time he came home from boarding school. Now he had chucked up school. With the war on he intended to get out into the world, and like so many of his forbears, probably emigrate to America. Meanwhile he had joined up; next month he'd be in the British Navy—his papers had just come. The coastguard job was only a full-time because he lived so handy and knew every inch of this coast.

But Shian? What would become of Shian, I asked.

Her brother looked troubled, but shrugged his shoulders.

"Sure, I worry at times about her," he said, choosing his words more deliberately. "But I guess she ought to be all right. The trouble is, she loves this place . . .

She's mad about the sea, you know. I don't think she'd be happy away from Kilcalla, she's never known any other home. I'm sure she'd mope and pine away if she had to leave here. She's perfectly happy so long as she can get to the sea every day. She's not the usual sort of girl—not likely! In a way she's queer, very queer. You'd be surprised if I told you she can tame wild animals? But it's true. She talks with them, and I've seen her actually stroking deer. And when she swims down there in the bay, she plays with the young seals!"

Brendan stopped, as if he had said too much. He got slowly to his feet.

"I must be going, sir. I oughtn't to have kept you talking so much. Only you . . . you seemed so interested in us."

"Of course I am," I put in hurriedly. "But tell me one more thing—I shall keep wondering if you don't. You say your sister is seventeen? Will you leave Shian alone here during the rest of the war, with only the old people and the . . . the inefficient bailiff? It seems to me—forgive my saying so—that your sister will only grow wilder and more difficult. You say that she will have nothing to do with the farm, and leaves everything to the bailiff, even the care of the grandparents? Couldn't I help in some way? I have a sister in London who would be pleased to give Shian a home and train her for some useful work . . ."

"Train her!" Brendan almost growled. "You don't think I haven't long ago suggested she did some useful war work! She laughs the idea to scorn. 'Let the British fight their own wars!' is all she says. As for keeping her in order—impossible! She's a year older than I am, anyway. No, you could never do anything with her. She's got her animals, her goats and seals, and all the wild notions our grandmother fixed in her silly head, and she'll never change. Never in this world!"

It seemed final. I stood up. The wind was backing to the north. Gerald would be in a rare mood by now. But still I was dissatisfied with the information about Shian. If only I could see her, for myself, and allay my intense curiosity about this wild child of nature. I remembered my vivid dream, in which the goat-child had seemed to be demanding something of me . . .

"Well, I must leave. But if I can help you at any time, here's my address. If you ever need any assistance, let me know. Don't hesitate to write. The story of Kilcalla has fascinated me, and one day I'd like to come back and explore this beautiful coast."

I held out my hand.

"You are welcome," he shook my hand, and then, to my surprise, blurted out hurriedly: "Look, sir, I feel I can trust you . . . It's God's truth, I am worried about Shian. It would be the best thing for her if she did go to London and work there. I'll speak to her, and ask her to write to your address. But I doubt she'll go. She's almost completely wild these days. She hardly ever comes home now. She doesn't seem to need food—not the sort up at Kilcalla house; she eats all sorts of wild foods. She does milk the goats—and leaves the milk in the dairy for the old folk—yes, she does do that much. But nothing else now. She spends all her time in the woods, and most of it here on the cliffs, or in the sea. She swims for hours—alone with the seals. Of course, we were always good swimmers—the whole family, for generations, were known as great swimmers. Grandmother herself was once a wonderful swimmer. Grandfather always boasts about her long distance swimming. But Shian beats us all. Yes, I admit—I am a good deal worried about my sister. I tell her that at her age—to go on like that—and in war time too! But it's no good . . . I can't persuade her to alter her queer habits. She's so much older and wiser than I, in some ways; and yet she's utterly childish and foolish in others. If only she didn't cling to these awful fancies of hers . . ."

He paused, and after a moment I said: "Tell me more about these fancies. I . . . I may be able to help you—and her?"

"I—I hardly like to, really, sir. Sure, they're quite daft! Well, for one thing, her main fancy is that she belongs to the sea. Grandmother ought not to have told her such a fairy tale really, but she did, and it's stuck with Shian ever since she can remember. When Shian was—well, it's too silly to repeat . . ."

"Go on," I begged him.

"When Shian was old enough to think for herself she asked grandmother what her mother was like. But grandmother used to smile secretly and say nothing, and grandfather would laugh. When at last Shian got an answer it was such a strange one that . . . that . . ."

Brendan hesitated, and I urged him to go on.

"Well, Shian has believed it ever since; and I'm afraid that our grandparents encouraged her because they had grown to believe the fairy tale themselves. At least they would never tell us where her parents came from. When I tried to be serious with them they would look at me and smile mysteriously, even chuckle like conspirators. 'You're an O'Malley all right,' they would say. But with Shian they always told her the same fairy tale."

"Fairy tale?"

"Simply this—they said that they had found her as a new-born baby in a seal cave on the beach when hauling timber there after a big storm one day in August! A few days before there had been a wreck, and some sailors drowned, and the Kilcalla people had been down on the Strand after what they could find— they were always a tough beachcombing lot. But as for this story of finding her as a new-born baby in a cave, and calling her their sea-princess—sure, it's a load of rubbish! They have filled her head with the crazy idea that one day when she grows up a sea-prince will come out of the sea and claim her, and carry her off to where she came from—the kingdom beyond the horizon! There—that's the story she believes in—and lives by!"

Brendan paused again, then went on quickly:

"Sure, I don't quite know why I tell you this, but it's a comfort to open my mouth wide for once to an intelligent person, sir. I dare not say anything in the village. It's already supposed that my sister is half-wild and half-mad. There are rumors about her sanity, and once the priest came to see if she oughtn't to be put in a convent—to calm her down. But if Shian is wild, she's not mad—she can be very intelligent, and she's a born naturalist. She only has this fancy about the sea and all it means to her—well, everything. It's really very wrong of our grandparents to keep up the story as if it were the truth; but as I say, grandmother and grandfather have talked themselves into believing it, too; year in and year out they have stuck to the story. And as for Shian, I know that she thinks about it all the time, even more and more now as she gets older and is trying to discover some meaning to her present wild existence. It sort of comforts her now, I believe."

I did not know what to answer—the whole story was so fantastic. For the sake of saying something, I asked where Shian had learned her singing, and also I was curious about this.

"From grandmother. We both learned reading, writing, books and singing—from grandmother. She was a wonderful woman until she had a stroke three years ago. She was well educated, but given to reading too much. She knew all the old Irish fairy tales, the tales of the leprechauns and fairies, and I really believe she had some sort of supernatural power. She was rather like Shian when she was young, I suppose, and knew the Kilcalla Strand about as well. But as for the yarn about Shian being found as a *mor-lo,* a sea-child in a seal cave—well, sure, I think it's only because Shian is so sunburnt and dark and such a lover of the sea—almost like a seal she is in the water—that the fancy came to grandmother, and she liked it so well that she's stuck to it until it's become the truth to her. Grandmother loved mystery and legend and every kind of superstition."

"But Shian is your sister, isn't she?" I asked after a pause. We had started down the cliffs toward the beach.

"Yes, I suppose so! At least she bears the same surname! We are O'Malleys. But she is quite unlike me, you know. She's small and dark, and has deep brown, almost black eyes and hair. You couldn't tell that we were brother and sister just by looking at us. Sometimes I really wonder, because grandmother would never admit we were. Shian's the dark Irish type, like the Iberian women who married our Scandinavian ancestors, they say. But I am more like the Norsemen, grandfather used to tell me."

There was no time to learn more. Brendan led me by a good path quickly through the great escarpment over which I had scrambled at random earlier. We hurried now, for a heavy swell was roaring on the beach and Gerald stood well offshore, anchor up and motor running. Already the waves were too big for the dinghy. I knew I should have to swim for it.

It was clear to me that Brendan was intelligent. His unusual upbringing and education at Kilcalla had given him the manners and speech of gentlefolk; and he had acquired or inherited a dignity and honesty worthy of princes. I longed to help brother and sister. I told him that I would see that he had all the advantages I could secure for him by recommendation when he entered the Navy next month. He was eager to take up my suggestion of some training in Naval Intelligence. In reply to my request for more information as to his education, I was not greatly surprised to hear that he had read the Icelandic sagas untranslated—thanks to his grandmother's interest in the subject. He had learned something of astronomy from his grandfather; this would be useful in perfecting the course in navigation which would be part of his training in the Navy. His command of English was perfect, although his accent was broadly Irish.

The sea broke with a harsh roar on the slate pebbles. It had lost the gentleness of early morning. It flung the stones clattering upon a long ridge which it pushed forward with hard blows as the tide rose. I saw that seals were swimming in the white-laced edge of the seaward breakers, their brown heads turned inquisitively toward us. Our motor boat with its dummy registration fishing mark "VW" stood a hundred yards off shore, too far for Gerald's shouts to reach me above the noise of the waves.

"What will you do?" asked Brendan anxiously. "The dinghy will hardly get through those breakers?"

I signalled with my arms, using Morse code: SWIMMING FOR IT.

I transferred my wallet to its waterproof sheath, and thrust it into my trousers pocket. I tied my shoes and coat tightly to the back of my belt, and said goodbye. Brendan had promised to write. I had promised to urge his acceptance—at Whitehall—as a recruit to the Naval Intelligence Division.

"Look here, sir. I'm a good swimmer," Brendan volunteered anxiously. "I'll swim out and get a rope, bring it ashore and get you pulled across to the boat. It's a long swim. The sea's getting rougher every minute."

"Thanks," I said, quite moved by the offer, "but I can make the same boast. I'm a good swimmer myself; and I'll have the wind with me. I'll be out there in a few minutes. Just watch!"

I ran into the incoming wave and dived through its cool white-veined arc. The next instant I was measuring with a long overarm stroke the gap between boat and beach. The whiskered faces of several seals bobbed up to look curiously at me, unsure if I were friend or foe. There were, I noted, some large-headed bulls among them—fellows with huge iron-gray hound-like profiles and thick battle-scarred necks that did not encourage me to linger. They stared hard, snorted fiercely, and then dived in my direction. I increased my pace.

One of the biggest males suddenly surfaced alongside me. His loud puff of watery breath startled and frightened me.

He was following too closely. His powerful male odor sickened in my nostrils, as he stretched his neck to get my scent. His eyes were bulging and bleary. I grew anxious, about as anxious as I might be alone in the middle of an empty field with a vicious bull.

When the great beast dived again, he rasped against my legs with his huge body. I knew I must do something to discourage his dangerous inquisitiveness. As he came up once more I turned swiftly and thumped the surface of the water with my flat palm—the alarm signal of the seals. The plan worked. I had a close-up view of the yellowish fangs displayed in a snarl of fear, the huge snout wrinkled and adorned with stiff white whiskers. Then he lurched over backwards in a ponderous somersault, and disappeared with a violent flick of his long-clawed tail-flippers.

I swam on watchfully. I judged myself to be about fifty yards from the boat, which now rose in full view on the swell, and then vanished again in the trough of the waves. I had a glimpse of Gerald standing amidships, a rifle pointed in my direction. He, too, had his eye on the bull seals!

He dragged me over the gunwale at last, with curses to hide his anxiety. He ran to thrust the engine into gear.

"Only just in time, you damn fool! My God, you've given me a rough go of it here! Where the hell did you get to? If you wanted to see that girl it would have been better to have stayed with me!"

"What d'you mean?" I asked in amazement.

"Look over there! In the midst of those seals!"

He pointed to a group of seals' heads about forty yards astern of us. I could see nothing but their brown bobbing forms on the white-streaked blue and green surface.

"There's the girl; can't you see her long hair?"

I was rubbing the salt out of my eyes and could not get a clear view.

"Why, she's been here half the morning, swimming and diving around while you've been chasing about on the dry land! I've never seen anyone swim so well. She came right up to the boat once and asked who I was. Dammit, man, I believe she's a mermaid or something very near it. She wouldn't come aboard, though I asked her to. I tell you she must be half seal anyway—only that I saw her legs, mighty fine legs too. Or am I dreaming? We'd better get out of this confounded place as quick as possible!"

"But I can't see anyone, Gerald. Where d'you see her now?"

"I don't. She's dived again, I suppose. Wait . . . no, that's only a young seal. Look out for a human face with flowing black pigtails . . . By the way, who is that fellow on the beach, a coastguard by the look of him? He's waving to you."

The boat was gathering way. I threw my arm high in a farewell salute to Brendan.

But even as I did so I saw a blacker head rise among the brown heads of the seals, and two black lines flowing over a pale neck and shoulders. For an instant the head turned to look at us, and although it was far away and almost shrouded with salt mist I knew it was Shian.

A few seconds later the marbled crest of a surf wave carried her upon the beach. As it receded she rose and stepped up beside her brother. Her ragged blue dress, wet and glistening, clung to the contours of her slender form. She turned to stare at us.

She did not wave.

But now the wind and the motor were driving us rapidly from the great wild theater of Kilcalla Strand.

As I moved forward to reef and hoist the sail I had a last glimpse of the two figures standing as if carved upon the shore. Slowly they faded from sight as the distance increased—as the salt spray, torn from the waves by the north wind, drew a curtain over the lonely land.

Chapter Two

It is next for me to tell how I came back to Kilcalla, and to record the strange adventures which caused me to leave behind my normal quiet and monotonous life attending to the family business in London, and be plunged into an existence so beautiful and yet so desperate that even today I tremble at the memory of it. But as others smile and hint that it must have been a trick of the imagination, or a fantasy dreamed in the long and idle holidays following my convalescence from war wounds—holidays which they knew I had spent in Ireland—I have ceased to speak of it. It is better to put down the truth of the whole experience in black and white, a task far more simple than might be expected, for each moment I spent in the far west is vivid in my mind as I write this.

It was six months after leaving him on the strand at Kilcalla that I met Brendan again. I had recommended him to the Naval Intelligence Division which, already short of good men, sought for youngsters of his caliber, particularly with his knowledge of the sea, and asked no questions about his Irish origin. In no time he passed his exams and tests in training for pilotage and commando tasks in small boats. There came to me an order to ferret out a suspected enemy submarine refueling base in a "neutral" country across the English Channel. In making up my crew for the big fishing smack which we were to use to hide our identity I asked for Brendan. He accepted at once, with great eagerness. He was to remain with me until he was killed in the landings in France. Ah, Brendan . . . a fearless man, and a noble companion to share a watch at sea!

In our patrols over many months there were chances for me to talk with Brendan. Gradually I learned almost all there was for me to know about the strange household of Kilcalla, about that extraordinary couple who were the grandparents, said to be the last mating of two lines of hereditary princedoms in all Ireland. As far as I could trace the genealogical records, this could have been true. Certainly the picture Brendan gave me of the grandmother convinced me of her aristocratic nature and powerful autocratic behavior. She dominated the Kilcalla scene. It was clear that her strength of will and tremendous imagination had put a spell, in childhood, upon Shian. Shian was small, perfectly formed, but dark, almost seal-like, not an O'Malley at all in appearance; and evidently the self-willed Grandmother O'Malley, come from a different line of tribal blood, had, for her own dark reasons, convinced the child of her daughter that she was of supernatural birth. And now it was too late. After her stroke Grace O'Malley had rejected Shian, leaving the girl spellbound.

These things I learned in the long intimate conversations with her brother. Then one day, over a year later it must have been, we made a pact between us.

It was just before the full-scale invasion of the French coast, in which we had a special diversionary part. At that moment we were dressed for a rehearsal in our life-jackets, I remember. It was to be a highly dangerous mission for our crew—a raid into a small enemy-held port by night—a vital part of the whole pattern of surprise ... Brendan's problem that day, and mine, was every man's problem. What would become of our dependants at home, if ... ?

By some strange psychic sense Brendan knew he would not survive the war. He did not fear death; but he was quite convinced that he had said goodbye forever to Shian. And she, too, he said, was equally sure they would never meet again on this earth.

Although I told him that I did not accept his fatalism, we there and then vowed to each other that if one was killed the survivor would seek out the people of the other, and give such help and comfort as was in our power, in case of need.

Shian still ran wild in the wilderness of Kilcalla; and Brendan was much relieved by my assurance that I would go there—if I were the survivor.

It so happened that Brendan was with the first wave of commandos to seize and keep open the dock-gates of the French port for the entry of the barge of explosives. Two-thirds of us were killed, including Brendan and my shipmate Gerald; and the manner of their dying was worthy of the high courage of these sons of Ireland.

I had not been near Kilcalla since that first discovery of it with Gerald. Nor could I go there for two more years. My brief leave periods had allowed me no more than a rare weekend at home. The last year of the war found me in hospital, suffering from a wound in the throat which had turned septic. I suppose it had been touch and go, but at last the danger was over. The specialist assured me that I would soon be as healthy as ever, but I must take a long rest. For the present I must avoid speech as far as possible.

I was to learn why he had recommended silence. When I found that I had lost the power of uttering co-herent words, I consulted my old and trusted family physician. But all he would say was that he hoped that one day my throat would be strong enough to support an artificial aid to speech. And with this vague hope I had to be content, thinking myself lucky (as I remem-bered Brendan and Gerald and the host of the gallant fallen) to be alive at all.

Of course I had written to Shian. As soon as I had recovered consciousness in the hospital I had written to her grandfather with the news of Brendan's brave death. When I received no reply, I wrote to Shian. But no reply came to these and other letters I wrote, offer-ing help.

I grew impatient, walking restlessly in the hospital gardens, healthy enough in the rest of my body; but they would not let me leave until the septic condition of my larynx had cleared up. All this time I dreamed of the loveliness and peace of Kilcalla, and of the strange sea-loving Shian. Although I had never seen her close to, the glimpses I had had of her were exciting enough; and once Brendan, spurred by my incessant questions, had produced a photograph of his sister as a child of ten years, vividly attractive, with a dark eager face totally unlike the fair-haired Brendan. That miniature was now in my possession, for I had taken it from his wallet after his death. It would help me in what was now clearly my duty—to find and rescue Shian.

I was utterly weary of the stench of antiseptics, the endless poking in my throat. I had amused myself reading, and perfecting my knowledge of, Irish, which I had learned to speak during the long conversations with Gerald and Brendan at sea. But this bored me now, as spring approached and I longed to escape to the country and the sea. Day after day I exercised in the garden, and swam in the hospital pool.

It was late April when at last, after a week at home, the surgeon gave me permission to go away for a holiday, provided I took care of my throat and reported back at the first sign of a relapse.

For months I had pored over maps of south-western Eire. I had obtained the largest scale survey sheets, and now I knew the topography of Kilcalla by heart— on paper. A wild and beautiful country—the maps confirmed that! Kilcalla was marked as a group of buildings, including a derelict castle and a chapel, far from any neighbor, five miles from the nearest hamlet, and ten from the nearest railway—a one-track line wandering forlornly through the valleys of the Kerry mountains: and subsequently I found even this had ceased to function.

It was a gray wet evening in early May when I reached the hamlet. I was grudgingly granted a bed in a thatched cottage inn. There I heard repeated, with the usual lurid exaggeration and sinister details which local gossip might be expected to add, the story of the O'Malleys of Kilcalla. It seemed that the old folk had died, within a few hours of each other, a year ago.

They had been buried in the grounds of the roofless private chapel attached to the former "castle," and a great gathering, composed largely of the oldest people of the district, had paid homage to the last of their princes. No, the granddaughter, Shian O'Malley, had not been present. No one knew quite what had happened to her. It was rumored that she was still to be seen occasionally about the cliffs and the shore, but no one went there much now. The Civil Guard had made an extensive search for her after the death of the grandparents. But they had scoured that wilderness in vain. The property was now hers, since her brother had been killed in the war. Most people believed that Shian was dead, had been dead for at least three years. As for this rumor of her running wild in that wilderness, well, who knows? It was always a haunted place. He—my landlord—didn't believe she was alive. No one had seen her for more than a year. Most likely drowned, she was such a devil for the sea; all the O'Malleys had been. But there were such things as spirits, weren't there, returning to haunt such places . . . ?

The landlord rambled on, while I nodded encouragement. My throat condition prohibited speech. I had to write down my questions, which he had some difficulty reading by the indifferent light of an oil lamp.

What was to become of Kilcalla?

Well, O'Hara the bailiff was just about alive and kicking, but pretty feeble now. He still tended the white cattle, if you could call looking around them in the pony cart now and then really caring for them. He was much too old, though once he had been a real rodeo character. But they said he was suffering from loss of memory—delusions he had. One of his fancies was that he had to stay on until the heir, the grandson Brendan, came home from the Navy. You couldn't convince O'Hara—he'd been so fond of the boy—that Brendan was dead. Yes, he knew O'Hara well; and I listened to a long eulogy of this old man, evidently a highly respectable character, but a recluse who did not welcome visitors, "wouldn't talk to anyone at all, at all.

You couldn't really blame him, the way the Agricultural Board still pestered him. Wanted him to plough a quota of land for corn—at his age!"

Food in the towns up country and in England was still rationed ...

The gossiping voice of the ferrety unshaven landlord droned through the empty taproom as it loosened with the aid of the powerful local poteen which I plied him with.

It seemed that Shian must be dead. That would explain the silence with which my letters had been received. Yet it was odd that the bailiff had not sent them back, or posted me a line of acknowledgement to the address I had written on the back of each envelope. But I would not despair yet. The next thing was to interview O'Hara.

It was still raining when I set out next day on the five-mile walk along a rough cart track, which began by climbing over a steep bare hillside, until it reached a derelict cottage in a valley two miles farther on. Behind this farm the mature woods of Kilcalla seemed to hide the sea coast. Looking at the black mass of the distant trees shrouded with rain, I felt a coldness creeping over me. Fear that Shian had died, alone in that wilderness, came to me; then a memory of Brendan's violent death. As I sheltered under the dilapidated walls of the cottage, wet and miserable, I was overwhelmed with the futility of my journey.

Cold and shivering, I pushed forward on the lifting of the rainstorm. A track led past this farm and disappeared into the woods. There were cart-ruts and hoof-marks of horses along the grassy road. But the trees were closing in, young saplings were springing up in the center, and briars and branches pressed upon me from both sides. By the state of the track it looked as if O'Hara came along here not more than once a month in his horse and trap.

As I gained the deep wood the trees rose higher above my head. They assumed noble proportions, oaks and beeches predominating, with here and there a Scots fir. A squirrel came boldly to look at me when I passed through the darker shade of a spruce grove. This part of the Kilcalla forest had surely been planted by human agency—these conifers were not native to Ireland. Soon after I noticed a cedar which must have been two hundred years old, no doubt planted in the days when the estate had been a flourishing feudal kingdom—as Brendan had described. Nearby a tall eucalyptus spoke of the mildness of the climate—Lusitanian, to use the jargon of the botanist familiar to me.

I was no longer sad. The sun had appeared, glancing through the trellis of the archway of boughs. I followed the cart-track which rose and fell over the folds of the land in a seemingly endless line. Forest birds sang with the joy of spring. Under the tall beech trees the air was scented above the drifts of bluebells, where I had glimpses from time to time of deer.

Then the forest thinned out and presently a wide meadow opened, almost yellow with primroses and cowslips, here and there a great oak, beech or larch standing alone in the verdure of tender spring foliage. Over this sunlit park the track drove forward, then began to dip steeply into a grassy valley, where a great herd of white cattle grazed.

I saw that they were led by a venerable bull with immense black-tipped ivory horns and shaggy dewlap. Brendan had told me about the ancient bull which commanded the herd and, although almost blind, seemed ageless. Nor was I alarmed, for Brendan had said that the white bulls were harmless if you did not annoy them; and secondly I saw plenty of great trees whose low branches invited lofty sanctuary should the herd stampede in my direction!

They were beautiful, these animals. Their coats were snow-white, only their muzzles and the inside of their ears and horn-tips were jet black. Most of the cows had young calves, which they now called to heel as they trotted toward the old bull. Recognizing me as a stranger, they were forming a defensive position—as wild cattle will. Four or five senior bulls moved up to the front while the cows brought up the rear. There must have been two hundred head in the herd facing me, with the master bull in front. He was uneasy as he sensed my nearness, and swung his great head to and fro, wrinkling his moist black nose to catch my scent. He bellowed a warning, then pawed the grass with a slow dragging movement of one forefoot.

I waited under the protection of a great beech. Some minutes passed, and I saw that the beasts were losing interest in me, beginning to graze peacefully. They gradually spread in a loose group astride the track, and in order to pass them I had to make a detour, gliding from tree to tree inconspicuously until I could regain the road beyond.

Crowning the farther slope of the sheltered valley, the broken tower and ruins of a great mansion were partly hidden under the forest, which here resumed its sway. This I recognized as the former "castle" of the O'Malley's of Kilcalla. Brendan had told me it had been destroyed by the English in the days of that redoubtable clanswoman and self-styled Queen, Grace O'Malley, who, "powerful in galleys and seamen," proclaimed herself greater than her contemporary Queen Elizabeth the First of England, and was responsible for enlarging so much the O'Malley inheritance. She had lived here at Kilcalla for a while, long enough to marry its owner-chieftain and to dismiss him after she had confirmed herself in possession and presented him with an heir—an early ancestor of Brendan.

A thousand yards across a vast grassy field sprouting unkempt with young elms rooting their way from the forest edge, the "modern" Kilcalla House could be seen—a group of buildings brown-gray against some black pines. I hurried forward, my heart beating faster.

There was nothing structurally remarkable about this—it was just another superior type of Irish squire's house, adapted to farm needs. But its neglected appearance and uninhabited air seemed to speak of the several family deaths its owners had lately suffered. At one time, in the tradition of Irish farms generally, the buildings had been whitewashed; but that was many years ago, and nothing now remained of that whiteness except some streaks on the upper half—the lower half was splashed and mucked by cattle which had used the walls to shelter against. The slate roofs of the outbuildings were full of holes which showed the decaying rafters.

The house itself was so clad with moss and ivy that at first it was difficult to pick out the windows. Some indeed seemed to have been completely overgrown. The roof, even the chimneys, were smothered with ivy, some of it brown-white and dead. What had once been a garden enclosed within neat walls was broken open to the cattle, which had left muddy paths all around the house. They had also plucked the ivy leaves for a height of five feet around the walls. The main entrance doorway, above a flight of broad steps, was entirely overgrown with thick ivy stems.

I was discovered first by a fine blue-coated deerhound which came bounding toward me with a ferocious barking. When I offered to pat its shaggy head it resisted, drawing back with bared teeth, growling, the hair rising upon its nape. It had a cold gray eye with the iris almost white, a peculiarity which enhanced the sinister appearance of the place.

The dog retreated barking as I advanced until, around a corner of the house, I came to a side entrance, which stood open. A dwarf figure awaited me under the high lintel.

O'Hara was dressed in faded brown corduroy coat and breeches. He was excessively spare, and seemingly fragile, the thinness of his legs plain even under thick puttees. His face was immensely old-looking, the upper part drawn and wrinkled and the eyes almost hidden in deep sockets overhung with white brows; the lower part of his face was concealed by white moustaches and a beard which cascaded luxuriantly to his waist, where his left hand held it in place lest the wind blow it awry. The breeze teased his long white locks so that they danced upwards each side of the bald crown, adding a touch of wildness to the venerable face.

I offered my hand, but he ignored this gesture.

"You are from the Agricultural Board?" he said abruptly.

I shook my head vigorously, and put my hand in my pocket, feeling for my list of questions, which I had prepared the night before.

"Then what do you want?" he asked, with a further compression of the crows' feet about his eyes. His voice was hostile.

As I could not speak, he repeated his first question, this time with an impatient ring in his hoarse voice. I dragged out my notebook, tore the first page off, and thrust it before him. On it was written:

"I am a friend of Brendan O'Malley. We were shipmates in the Navy. He was killed in the same action in which I was wounded in the throat. I am dumb as a result. But I promised Brendan I would visit Kilcalla, and offer all the help I could."

The dog growled as I handed the message to the bailiff. He motioned it to be quiet and took the paper. He fumbled in his pocket. Not seeming to find what he wanted, he curtly bade me wait; then, pushing the dog outside to keep watch on me, he went within and slammed the heavy door upon us.

This was not exactly the true Irish hospitality, I reflected grimly, but I remembered Brendan's warning that if ever I went to Kilcalla and met O'Hara I was to ignore his brusque manner which hid a generous heart and deep love of the estate; also Brendan had said the old bailiff was excessively suspicious of late, and seemed to live in the past almost as much as his grandparents had.

The hound growled and got ready to spring at my throat when I moved restlessly, examining the moldy facade of the house. There was nothing to do but wait. The sun was shining through the light swirl of sea-fret over the tree-tops. I heard anew thrushes and blackbirds singing in the woods and ruined gardens.

From the house came only faint sounds as of someone moving about, and the scraping of a chair. It seemed to me I had stood there, cold and wet, for half an hour before the door opened and O'Hara motioned me to enter.

His attitude was more gracious now. He led me

through an empty dairy to a wide stone-flagged kitchen. At the far end was a great inglenook with a hearth on which logs burned freshly. He took my coat and bade me warm myself. A black gallon kettle was singing as it swung on a gallows over the fire. A long table with benches occupied the center of the floor. A grandfather clock and a tall dresser filled with old china stood against the wall opposite the windows. Brass pots and copper pans, tarnished with neglect, adorned a wide shelf above the lintel of the ingle, close beneath a hanging bacon-rack. Dust and cobwebs festooned the walls and ceiling, but the middle of the kitchen was clean, as if it had just been swept. A lamp hung from a beam, helping to lighten a room darkened by the ivy which obscured much of the window-glass.

"I fear our hospitality is not what it used to be. I can offer you some tea?"

O'Hara threw more logs on the fire, and signed to me to sit on the skew beside the fire.

It would be tedious to give a full account of how we communicated that afternoon. It was a curious exchange of question and answer. For O'Hara was short-sighted, and I quite dumb; thus the only means of intelligible communication was for me to write my part—which O'Hara read with the help of pince-nez spectacles; and for him to speak his, which he did very slowly, with pregnant pauses.

When I had explained that I had first seen Brendan and Shian years ago on Kilcalla Strand; and when he had realized that Brendan and I had been together throughout Brendan's service in action with the Navy, he became more communicative, and the main points of our conversation—if such it may be called—were made as follows:

O'Hara: "It is surely hard for me to believe that I shall see Master Brendan no more."

I wrote down: "He covered himself with glory by his great courage in attacking a machine-gun post single-handed. He died like a true chieftain of Ireland."

"I knew it in my heart, for after a long time I thought I should open and read your letters to the old man and to Miss Shian ... but somehow I could not allow myself to give up hope altogether."

"Did Shian read my letters?"

"She has read nothing since Master Brendan stopped writing to her ... you know she has second sight, that girl. As soon as Master Brendan went to the war, she knew that he would never return ... alive. She told me this the very moment he left."

"I came here because I promised Brendan, if he died, to help his people," I wrote down, returning to my first explanation. "For he had promised to help mine if he lived and I died. It was an agreement between shipmates. I could not come at once, because I had been wounded."

"His people are beyond mortal help." He crossed himself and muttered: "God and Mary the Mother of Jesus be with them."

"But most of all I promised I would visit and help his sister Shian. Surely she is not dead?"

The old man stared a long time at my question, as if by reading it over and over he could gain time to think out a proper answer. He looked earnestly at me afterwards, but said not a word. The suspense was terrible.

I jerked his sleeve.

"No," he said heavily at last, "she is not dead. She was here yesterday."

My heart gave a vast leap within me, and my face must have shown my joy, for he shook his head and added:

"But she might as well be dead. I can do absolutely nothing with her. She is completely wild and has partly lost her reason."

My anxious look invited a more detailed explanation, and slowly and painfully he gave it:

"Shian was always wild. Her grandmother believed she was born of the sea-folk, and I—you would laugh if I told you that I—too believe it now, although I did not at first. I was once a sensible sort of fellow, like any well-trained bailiff. I loved my master and mistress, and I was proud of them. They loved me in their way, too, the way of noble people who are conscious that

39

their royal blood required of them generosity and tolerance as well as leadership. I helped to teach Master Brendan what he knew of the outdoors and farming. I taught him to ride and to race blood horses, for once I was a great rider myself. But Shian ... there was no need to teach her anything; except to look at she was a true O'Malley, born to the open air, to the saddle, to the chase, to tree-climbing, to swimming, to every outdoor activity, and, above all, this passion for the sea. I liked all these things myself once, and could enjoy their delight in them when they were both very young. But Shian went too far—she soon got out of hand—she was high-spirited and spoiled by her grandmother, who encouraged her to run wild, and loved to hear Shian's stories of her adventures in the forest and in the sea. Many a day have I heard them talking together so—so wildly, of the woods and the sea ... Shian became uncontrollable at an early age. She never went to school—learned her reading and writing and singing from her grandmother. Then one day her grandmother had a stroke, after falling down the stairs. The grand old lady Grace O'Malley was unconscious for a week, and when she recovered she could remember very little of the past. She became like a child, even worse than her husband, who was twelve years older and already very feeble with age. Shian watched over her during the week she lay as if dead, only to get a terrible shock when her grandmother, on waking, failed to remember her at all. She never recovered her memory and would stare at Shian almost you might say with displeasure, and when Shian pleaded she would ask her to go away and not bother her."

I had heard this story from Brendan, and its accurate repetition from O'Hara would have convinced me, had I needed to be, of the sincerity and devotion of the old bailiff. I urged him to tell me more of Shian's present state of mind.

"She rarely comes to the house now, only when she wants something, and I am not always here when she calls. In fact, I think she deliberately avoids me. Yesterday she came to get some clothes. She was in the last rags, her garments torn with her wild life in the woods and the sea, more than half naked. I tried to reason with her. Again I told her it was her duty to help me settle the estate. I have tried to talk with her so often. But it is useless. You might as well talk to the birds of the air or the seals of the sea, for she is like both. She is like a wild animal in the house, longing to escape. It was only because of the dog barking to welcome her yesterday that I knew she had crept into the house. And when I heard her rummaging in the clothes' chests upstairs, in desperation I locked the doors so as to try to hold her and reason with her for the last time."

The old man was slumped in his seat in deep dejection.

"When she found the doors locked she was mighty angry. I have seen that wild anger of the O'Malleys before. She demanded that I should open the door or she would smash it down. I begged her on my knees to tell me for the last time what I must do with the estate—for it is all hers by right of inheritance.

" 'Do what you like with it!' she stormed at last. 'It's yours—keep it for yourself! What good is it to me?' and she laughed so wildly that I felt sure her reason was going. I begged her to tell me what she intended to do with herself, but she only went on laughing hysterically. I think she has reached the point of loathing this old house. She is really frightened of the place. The memory of her grandmother's stroke and death haunts her yet."

He paused for so long that I had to pluck his sleeve again.

"Yes, surely she hates this place . . . all her people have died now. She thinks it's haunted by evil spirits. That's why she would set it on fire if she could . . . if only I was not living here to stop her."

Again he paused, and again I touched his sleeve before he resumed:

"She took a brand from the hearth yesterday and offered to set the place on fire! 'If you don't want it, let's burn it! I'll never come here again, O'Hara!' she screamed; and threw the brand into that pile of kindling wood—over there!"

I nodded dumbly, with a tight feeling in my throat.

"She must be insane, but there it is ... I could only unlock the door and let her go, and then hurry back and put out the fire."

He stopped, and I wrote down: "Where is she now?"

"She came back almost immediately," O'Hara continued, "but only as far as the garden wall, in answer to my hand whistle—an old family signal—which I had given from the door in a last attempt to win her attention. She always seems more rational out of doors. And indeed, afterwards we had what you might call almost a sane conversation."

Again he stopped, and I had to write down: "What did she say to you?"

"She actually apologized for losing her temper. She was crying, poor child. But she was quite determined, she said, to have nothing more to do with the estate. Then by degrees I discovered that she was still obsessed with that incredible fairy tale of her grandmother's, that she must be ready for ... but why should I go on? It's just a load of nonsense that's fixed in her pretty head. She's deranged. What in God's name can I do?"

"Brendan told me something about these odd fancies Shian has," I wrote down hurriedly. "But I can only help if you tell me *everything* please." I underlined the word.

Shaking his head dubiously he told me that Shian believed she was under a spell! She still believed the old story and prophecy her grandmother had instilled in her from childhood, the fairy tale of a prince of her own blood, a man of the sea-folk, who was coming to take her away from Kilcalla, away to some beautiful world beyond the sea where she would be happy ever after ...

"Yes," he cackled derisively, before resuming a grave face, "that much I learned again yesterday, though not in any direct words from her. She never mentioned her fairy prince—but I did. She referred to her grandmother's tales which, alas, I had myself encouraged in idle moments of talking to her as a child. This western land is full of legends and stories of mermaids and mermen . . . and now I once more tried to undo the mischief we had encouraged her to believe in as a child. I told her she was no longer a foolish girl, it was time for her to give up these ridiculous notions and behave like a sensible woman. But it was no good. She was—she remains—quite obsessed . . . Ah, I know that young woman all too well. For all her mad ways, she has great skill and wisdom, and an ability to thrive and be perfectly happy under the open sky. I don't blame her for hating this gloomy old place. I have begun to loathe it myself . . ."

He was pitfully hunched in his seat as he finished:

"That girl has second sight, undoubtedly. For she told me yesterday that she knew I had planned to leave Kilcalla for good, though I have told nobody she could have seen—and she sees nobody at all. I gathered that she had come back to the house for two reasons: to say goodbye forever to me, and to obtain some fresh clothes for the last time—in readiness for meeting her sea-prince! She has done both . . ."

As he stood up, swaying a little, he added in Irish, as if to himself: "And that's the last I shall see of Shian O'Malley! She said so herself!"

He spread the embers of the hearth, to let the fire die out, saying he was leaving right away. "I am too old for all this now," he sighed pathetically. "I have done all I can for her, and the estate, and now I am going to give up. When you came today I had already packed my things. If you want a ride to the inn you can come along with me. I am going to arrange with the lawyers for the disposal in trust of the whole estate. I shall not return to Kilcalla to live any more, though I shall have to visit it to see to the white cattle until something is decided about the herd."

I took up my pencil and wrote down: "How can I help you and Shian? Have you any suggestions?"

"None," he answered wearily. "The whole thing is beyond help. We can do no more."

I detained him, writing down: "But I *must* find Shian and try to reason with her."

At this even O'Hara, gentle soul as he was, laughed sarcastically.

"How can you reason with her if you are dumb? In any case, if the Civil Guards can't find her after a month of combing the woods and the shore you're not likely to run her to earth."

These points went home. But I was not in a mood to be discouraged. I argued with him for a while longer, with my bits of scribbled paper, but he was thoroughly pessimistic. It was quite useless, he said.

We went out to put the horse in the trap.

Yet one gleam of hope had come to me during the afternoon. O'Hara had said casually, but with heavy sarcasm, that if some young man could pretend to be a prince of the sea, one of the legendary merfolk, and swim ashore upon the great strand of Kilcalla where Shian spent almost all her time, he might find her waiting to welcome him!

That purely jesting and bitter remark stuck in my mind.

We arrived late that night at the inn. In the morning we parted early. O'Hara had given me his address, and his blessing in case I really embarked on my search for Shian. But clearly he believed my quest was hopeless.

Chapter Three

If only I had the power to describe the majesty of the dawn of the day on which I sailed for the Kilcalla Strand! It seemed to me that the sky had never held such an armada of multi-colored clouds which, long before the sun rose, came advancing, galleon after galleon, out of the darkness of the south-west. Very beautiful and beyond words to describe—but wild and sinister too.

For two days I had been busy preparing for the voyage. I had stayed in the nearest seaport, talking with the fishermen and loungers by the quayside. I let it be known that I wanted to buy a small boat and take it by easy stages up the coast as far as Valentia . . .

They appeared to be well satisfied with the price I gave for the boat which I ultimately chose. The bargain after all was all on their side. I knew that it was a miserable shell, not worth a quarter of what I paid for her. The sly old fisherman who sold her praised her up to the skies while his comrades, frequently turning their heads aside to grin, nodded their agreement.

They were more than satisfied, the seller and his accomplices, when I, the dumb greenhorn, entertained them in the tavern when the deal was clinched. Thus I became owner of this rotten dinghy whose cracked timbers and patched boards were so cunningly smoothed over with a glossy new coat of paint.

Well I knew that her worm-eaten mast would scarcely stand up to a stiff breeze, even should the ancient linen sail hold the wind for more than a dozen healthy puffs. Yes, they were well satisfied and gave me many assurances of the sea-worthiness of this wretched tub. At the same time they warned me of the difficulties of the passage, of the strength of the wind and the tides between here and Valentia. They advised me, with genuine anxiety now, to keep close inshore all the way and not to venture out from the land unless the sea was perfectly quiet. The queer silent tourist must not be allowed to drown himself . . .

At the end of the following day the strong north wind had died away. That night a thick sea-mist came up from the west, bringing warm air and a promise of southerly winds and cyclonic weather. The fishermen told me that I had better delay my journey, as they smelt mischief in the sudden change. The glass was low, they said. But I made it known that as the night was dead calm, I would leave before dawn, if no wind got up meanwhile.

At three the next morning my dinghy was well clear of the breakwater before the mist and the night had lifted. I had pulled away eagerly, anxious to get to sea unseen, and to put the first headland, the tumbled rocks of Horse Island, between me and curious human eyes.

The cry of nesting gulls on the island cliffs gave me the clue as to my exact position had I been in any doubt. I could barely see the outline of the land and the faint white surf singing against the steep reefs.

Soon the increasing movement of the boat warned me that I was entering the first of several tide-races between me and my far-off destination. But I was unconcerned, happy in the hope of a swift passage; for I had so planned those morning hours to take advantage of the current. It was in my favor, so far. Dawn was breaking.

The sailor within me knew that the crimson shield in the eastern sky foretold a storm. The wind began to whisper urgently upon my left cheek as I stepped the mast, taking care to stay her well with the new cords which I had brought. Then I raised the flimsy lug-sail, which I had patched in its weakest place with linen thread. At once the little shallop bounded forward, willingly, eagerly. I trimmed the boat well by placing the oars conveniently. I baled out the water, which spurted in freely, when she lurched, from cracks above her water line. I knew it could not be long before the old canvas of the sail split, but I had prepared for that. Once the wind became strong enough to destroy this sail I should put up a new storm trysail, which was bundled in my haversack.

If possible I intended to keep that trysail, and use it as my tent ashore, while seeking for Shian . . .

We were scudding along fairly smoothly now, before a freshening south-east breeze. My left hand was quietly upon the tiller. The wind and the tide were as one, racing in the right direction with me. Only a few awkward white breakers here and there intercepted us. She slapped through these and groaned and creaked as she danced about for a drunken moment or two.

Well it suited my purpose—this crazy boat which I should divest myself of at the right second. But meanwhile I had to be careful not to precipitate matters by encountering white water too soon. I kept her about a mile offshore, aiming for the loom of the Kilcalla mountain which marked my goal beyond the next promontory.

I was content with my success so far. I was enjoying myself, as always in a small boat. And I was far from lonely.

Looking back I saw that the tireless-winged fulmars (these Arctic birds nested on Irish cliffs now) were following me, circling in long ellipses. I saw the snow-white face of the petrel, with the warm mysterious dark-rimmed velvety eye, close to me as one swooped past. Fishermen call them "mollies," and believe each is inhabited by the soul of a drowned sailor. In the unblinking gaze of that handsome eye I seemed to read some message, some warning . . .

When the sun rose, its roseate light flickered here and there on the open heaving sea, as if a searchlight were sending me another message, a warning not to play the fool, and to get back to the safety of the land.

Black clouds re-united over the blue patches in the sky. The waves suddenly became angry, attacking the boat at new angles. The mast lurched ominously and the first rent opened in the ancient rag of the sail.

The white-faced cormorants came heading in from the open sea, their ghoulish bodies floating easily in the strong wind as they aimed for the isolated Toor Rock, standing close ahead of my course. I saw how fast I was moving when we slipped past this sentinel. I was encouraged by our speed.

Suddenly there was a slashing tearing report. The Toor Rock formed behind it an eddy of wind and current which I ought to have anticipated. The boat was sucked sideways by the sea below, and buffeted by the wind above. In an instant the lug-sail hung in shreds on its yard. We swayed, close to capsize in the whirling race.

I felt surprisingly unalarmed. Discarding the torn canvas, and its yard, overboard, I unrolled the trysail, tied its foot to the bow-ring, and hauled the peak to the masthead. Then with the sheet in my hand I crawled to my seat in the stern, knee-deep in water. My only fear now was the rotten mast; the sail and cords were new, and would not break.

Then I baled her. She still made water rapidly, but I could gain on it, right hand using the scoop as my left hand held the tiller. We settled down again, my boat and I, upon this strange journey, still with a favorable current.

Many thoughts I had. It seemed as if I was living a dream. Could it be true that I was really embarked upon this desperate adventure, this hopeless journey in search of this spell-bound child of the sea, this ghost girl of Kilcalla?

But at every lurch we made over the swelling waves the mast creaked, "It's true!" And the black cliffs, rising higher and wilder as I drew nearer the menhir headland, frowned at me as if saying, "Go forward, fool! There's no turning back!"

The south-east gale drove me onward with an inevitability that calmed my mind. I remained watchful of each wave. When I luffed slightly to avoid white water breaking on a submerged rock the south-easter threw the boat on its beam ends. Only by a smart swing of the tiller did I save her from capsize.

Then I must bale and bale again, for once more the boat was full.

My oars had slipped overboard when we heeled over. But what did I care? We were racing straight for the southern horn of the Kilcalla bight, three miles away. This wind was a beautiful wind, almost a fair wind, yet not too fair to make steering and balance awkward. I had no fears for my trysail—if only the mast would hold. If only that long crack which had started to open on the port side where a rotten board had sprung from the ribs—if only that did not spread wider. I must help keep it above water by leaning more to starboard. But the waves were not so particular as to which side of the boat they slapped.

Surely I must be mad to care so little? Why, I was almost radiant with excitement and hope, enjoying the cruise hugely! How beautiful the sea was; yet growing darker every moment. Indigo clouds were rushing at us from the open ocean, shooting upwards toward the land at a frightful pace.

Well, it could not be long now. Provided the mast held, the wind and tide would carry us with them around the last headland. Then I should be ready to let the boat sink; and put into operation my plan . . .

Would Shian be waiting for me? Perhaps as she loved the wild moods of the sea, she would be playing with the storm waves on the strand? Again and again, from the moment of leaving harbor, this thought had tormented me, even as I enjoyed the wild leaping and crashing of the rotten shell of my boat toward her hiding place. For if I could not find her by this approach I would never find her.

I thought I knew this coast pretty well from a long study of the charts during my convalescence, although I had only once sailed inshore—in fine weather—that time with Gerald. The fishermen had warned me to keep clear of the long reef which ran out from this headland. Two miles away I could see more vividly the bar of white water there. I had thought it possible with the north-going tide to slip my shallow craft between a gap in this bar, close to the rocks, but now, at over a mile distant, I could see only a long unbroken wall of white overfalls.

No passage. I took a more westerly slant. But now I had to bale, faster and faster, for the lee beam curtsied to every wave, and the water poured in. The slightly different motion, sideways in the troughs of the waves, would snap the mast at any moment. For the boat to stay afloat I would have to find a passage further west. That I knew; but I remained calm, even exuberant.

We raced on. Baling faster now, I had also to swing the tiller more rapidly to avoid the fall of the biggest crests. The dancing water-logged dinghy responded marvelously—under the circumstances.

Although my head was cool, and my body chilled with the sharp wind and salt spray, my heart thumped a little faster. My thoughts still floated on air, like the fulmar which periodically glided over the mast, looking down upon the puny man and his absurd shell which had dared the strength of wind and tide. I knew from experience that in time of danger my brain could be quite clear. I concentrated upon finding a gap in the heaving white outfall which barred the entrance to Kilcalla Bay.

Two tides meet at this point. The north-going current clashes with the powerful south-moving stream which sweeps the inner bight of the Kilcalla Strand. There is no passage for a small boat in stormy weather through this conflict of the main tide with its counterforce, the eddy.

And what now? If there was no passage for my little craft, why struggle to get farther to sea? Better to aim straight for the shore, take the wind fair behind me, and gain at least a few more yards toward safety before we are swallowed up.

I swung the tiller to hold her before the wind, and noted that the gale had veered to the south-west and was bringing in a heavier swell. Already we were in the laced pattern of little breakers which curled and sidled at the towering snow-white outfall of the eddy tide.

To the right the jagged wall of the land's end rose black and menacing, with its huge menhirs. To the left, in the west, the storm clouds were inspissated, gathering upon us with a solid wall of sleet. Thus imprisoned, between the devil of the reef and the inhospitability of the cruel sea, the little boat advanced into the maelstrom, now shooting forward like a surf rider, now checked by the backlash of a comber.

As we sank into the pit of a huge wave the mast snapped.

Yet still my mind was calm. This was the signal I had prepared myself for. In the last few minutes, waiting for the boat to break, I had thrown off my clothes, save my short trousers, my strong leather belt and its sheath knife. But I should have to abandon the trysail—my future tent—maybe it would be washed ashore?

As the fore part of the boat was overwhelmed I plunged quietly from the tilted stern into the towering crest of the wave. I began swimming with a slow deliberate stroke, saving my strength, taking a deep breath between each lift of the sea.

How warm the water was, after the cold wind! I was invigorated. But I was a little annoyed because the boat had failed me too soon. I had meant it to founder nearer the beach, which was not even in sight. It looked as if I should have a long struggle to win past the menhir point and enter the bight.

The fulmar petrel suddenly flew very close, once or twice dipping as if to touch my head with his oil-fouled bill. But I was very much alive. Reaching out suddenly I gathered the carrion-eater by one wing, and for an instant dragged him under water.

"That'll teach you, greedy old Mollemawk!" I shouted—but no words came.

He rose with a cackle, his plumage awry, and flew awkwardly away.

For a long time it seemed to me that I was making no headway. The white surges carried me forward, then sucked me back. Perhaps I swam for many hours. I do not know, for the timekeeper in the sky—the sun—was veiled by the sullen mauve sheet of the storm clouds. But as I swam I was careful to husband my strength, now and then treading water and drifting at ease.

I would not fight the current. In due course it would weaken and turn in my favor.

It seemed a very long time before, from the top of a larger billow, I sighted, afar off, the northern arm of the Kilcalla bight, that curving bastion at the far end of the escarpment. But as yet the pebbles of the strand were not in view. I was safe. I might relax now.

I was drifting, swimming languidly, with the turn of the tide as it began weakly to follow the wind toward the strand. Yes, I was tired now, in need of a longer rest. I turned over on my back and floated, rising and falling gently on the tireless green and white swell under the gray dome of heaven. Even as I marked the fall of the wind in the slow majestic halting of the clouds, I had time to think once again of the madness, the futility of this seeking of Shian. My wayward brain was confused for a moment, I could not work out clearly what I had planned to do next. I must not fall asleep!

When I felt rested enough, I began to swim steadily toward the shore, making for the spot where—years ago—I had last seen Shian. A mile away, at least?

I was too far to hear the roar of the waves on the strand yet. The only sounds were the hissing of the white horses which rode atop every hill of the sea, and a sigh when at the bottom of each swell the waters folded together.

I half closed my eyes against the incessant sting of the salt, as a mantle of foam caressed my body. Snowy bubbles wreathed my neck like the blossom of a tropical lei. When I rose up to gaze landwards again I saw that the current had helped me half a mile nearer inshore. I must be careful lest it carry me too far. With new strength I struck out for the pebbles, which now I could glimpse from the top of each wave, a thin blue line below the rain-filled escarpment.

I saw no soul awaiting me.

As I moved forward, straining my eyes, hoping,

hoping, I came upon the seals. They were always here—I remembered that now. And I remembered too a certain giant bull which had paid me far too much attention—on my first visit here. My hand went to my belt instinctively. My knife was safe in its sheath.

At first all seemed well. The seals were feeding, diving down to snatch the flatfish which the ground-swell was dragging from the sandy depths. They ate and played, gamboling among the gray-white dunes of the sea. I swam through their ranks, receiving only a cold stare. Strange, I thought to myself (for I am not a wild beast) that, watching the seals bite into the luscious white flesh of flounder and plaice, made me too feel hungry! I must have been swimming a long time, to feel hunger like that.

It was this sensation that made me involuntarily strike at a large skate which suddenly breached the surface near me. Now a skate normally never leaves the bed of the sea. But before I had time to realize, from the cloud of blood surrounding the fish, that this was not a normal occurrence—that this skate had already been half-eaten by a seal, I had already plunged my knife into its soft white underside. Thus far I got. What I should next have done with the skate I shall never know, for at that moment a heavy body struck me.

I felt the teeth of some great beast crunching through my left shoulder.

The weight of my attacker knocked the breath out of my lungs. He pressed me down. We sank together.

I cannot remember how I escaped from his vicious grip. I suppose my right hand, still holding my knife, must have swung around and the blade entered between the ribs of the master bull, for he it was who had attacked me.

He squirmed as my blade struck, and let go. With salt water in my lungs, I shot to the surface, choking, in a mist of blood and foam.

The wounded skate thrashed feebly on the surface. Beyond it suddenly shot up the head of the great bull. The brown bulging eyes were wide and white-ringed with his fury. He hurled himself out of the water upon me.

So the battle began.

I would willingly have left him to his skate in peace, but he was wounded and outraged. Was he jealous of me too? In his immense size, in the thick scarred folds of his neck and in his long ugly hound-like face he was the spit of the bull which I had encountered years ago. Now his roaring attracted the other seals. They gathered about us, lifting their heads out of the waves on all sides, curious spectators.

But my blood was hot too.

Maybe this great beast thought he would easily dispose of this spidery white human body? Hadn't he killed many a long-armed pale cuttlefish, whose clinging suckers embarrassed him only long enough for him to bite the huge cold eyes out of the creature?

As for me, I couldn't roar. My battle cry was choked in my dumb throat. But I met his bulk on the point of my knife. It was an old, true and tested blade. Nor was I an inexperienced diver and underwater hunter. As a naval cadet I had swum in coral lagoons, hunted for clams and even killed small sharks and large dog-fish with this same knife.

My left shoulder seemed paralysed, but my right side was still strong and I met the attack with a full thrust, striking below the bull's chin with all my strength. As he propelled himself upon me the blade went home in the tough blubber. It seemed not to reach a vital point—even with the second stab, which I had time to make before his teeth met in my left shoulder again.

We sank. This time I held my breath, remembering the trick taught in diving lessons.

The old bull hung on to my shoulder, wrenching and tearing, and crunching with his long fangs. My eyes were open but I could see nothing for the cloud of blood and the swirling of the sand upon the undertow of the swell.

My blade was still firm in my hand and I struck again and again. I was trying to find the seal's heart under the tough skin and thick fat. But he seemed to

54

be made of solid blubber. He hung on, wrenching savagely. I felt my shoulder cracking, but still I beat at him, and flailed, and drew my knife criss-cross about his breast, while his clawed flippers hugged me close.

My lungs were bursting. We rolled in the sand on the ocean bed.

Suddenly he relaxed. I was weak now. Not a drop of air left in my lungs. But my mouth was tight shut as I fought my way to the surface. There I lay gasping for a long while. The other seals made a ring around me, staring in wonder.

In the distance, as a wave lifted me on a pinnacle of crimson water, I saw another bloody ring, edged with brown heads. In its center floated a huge dark object, writhing convulsively. There would be no more trouble from the great bull, I hoped.

But now I, too, was weary unto death. I lay helpless, drifting upon the long dun swell. When I tried to swim forward I found I could barely use one arm. The other trailed loosely from my lacerated shoulder. Probably it was broken, but I was too numb to know.

I gave one last look around me. Already, attracted by the blood, the predatory gulls hovered close overhead. But in the eyes of the young seals which had surrounded me I thought I saw sympathy, before I closed mine in complete exhaustion.

Subconsciously I took and held a deep breath, to inflate my lungs with much-needed oxygen to keep me afloat, rocked in the gray-white cradle of the storm which had brought me here. How far I was from the strand I knew not. Nor could I care any more, for my whole body was without physical sensation. Instead I seemed to be floating on air at a great height as if I were a bird. In this fantasy I wandered in flight over the great wilderness of Kilcalla and its horizon of mountains. Below me I saw the forest spread before my feverish eyes, every detail more clear than on those maps I had pored over so long at home. How strange . . .

Thus I drifted.

I drifted through my disembodied dream, painlessly,

with increasingly sweet hallucination. Many hours, a whole day, seemed to pass in this blissful benumbed state.

Hush-ah! Hush-ah! Into my dreams slowly crept the gentle hushing of the sea as the storm abated, a dim lullaby mingling at last with an increasingly loud refrain as the waves carried me forward and crashed upon the slate pebbles.

Chapter Four

When at last I awoke I dared not, at first, open my eyes. I was afraid to destroy the illusion of stillness, peace and warmth. The music of the surf was faint in my ears. My shoulder was painful and stiff, but I knew I was at rest, and need not struggle any more. I was no longer tossed about by waves, or flying in imagination over the forest canopy. Something beautiful was happening—I was listening to a song, that self-same song which Gerald and I had heard years ago, on landing at Kilcalla.

First one verse, then another, came to me, in lilting Irish. As I listened, happiness stole into my heart through the melodious voice of a young woman telling the story of her own heart in song. I heard of the children of the sea, the habits of the sea-folk, of the caves where the calves were born, of their leader, who was a prince come from the ocean ... And after each descriptive verse, or two, the refrain:

Song of my heart, O Sea, thou art singing
Down there in the great strand thou are beating,
Thy music is under my head in the heather,
Thy music is in my ear when of thee I am dreaming,
For I have given my heart to the sea
*   and the folk of the sea.*

Later I was to write down a dozen of the five-line verses Shian would sing, which told the story of the sea people, mingled with her own longings and belief. I was to learn that song, although I could never sing it. The wound in my throat ... Yes, in due course I knew

57

almost every word, although Shian sometimes varied the theme, to match a new incident in our lives, a new thought that came to her. And sometimes she would add a whole new stanza to mark a special occasion.

Ah, Shian! It was you who rescued me as I drifted, a seeming corpse as the strong tide and the onshore wind carried me toward the pebbles. You had witnessed from the slope of the escarpment my fight with the master bull, having seen the commotion in the water as you were bringing your goats down to the strand! And in the defeat and death of the king of the seals at the hands of your "prince" (as you called me) was the fulfillment of the prophecy in your Song of the Sea.

Shian! It was you who swam out to my drifting body, who found me unconscious, while the cool waves washed my wounds, while I scarcely breathed. (Meanwhile the carcass of the great bull, drained by a dozen wounds, was being scavenged by those rival fishermen, the gulls and fulmars, as Shian pulled me the last few wave-lengths ashore.)

There on the strand she nursed me and bound my wounds, while the storm spent itself, and the sun came out to warm me. I slept long.

Slowly I opened my eyes, while my ears were filled with the music of the song, this Song of the Sea, which she sang as she stood between me and the strand. Her back was turned to me, and thus I saw her without her knowledge—at first. She was no longer a girl. She was a woman, though not of tall stature. I studied her strong brown legs placed firmly apart on the pebbles. Her short arms were crossed behind her back, as she gazed seawards. She wore a blue smock, which scarcely reached to her knees. There were no sleeves to hide the sun- and salt-browned arms. A leather belt drawn close to the slender waist supported a small sheathed knife. Her neck was concealed by a thick tangled mass of black hair which fell past her shoulders, and glistened as if still wet from the sea.

Presently she flexed her fingers, as if they were sticky with salt; and without turning around she brushed the back of one hand against the palm of the other, in a cleansing motion. It was then that I noticed a curious aberration.

Yes, I wanted to rub my eyes when I saw that between the long brown fingers were webs—very thin almost transparent, yet quite distinct, webs such as you may see joining the digits of the seal's flippers! And I saw, against the strong light, that they were mapped with the fine lines of numerous blood vessels. Later I was to know that hand, and how warm it was, even on the coldest day.

But just then I must confess that the discovery was a shock and caused a cold feeling to pass along my spine. Hitherto I thought I had been able to rationalize all the eccentricities I had heard from Brendan and O'Hara about this child of wild nature. But those webs! The more I pondered upon this unnatural fact the more disturbed I felt. (Much later I was to learn that a few people do have this aberration of webbed fingers and toes, but none so well developed as Shian's were.)

I must have moved slightly or groaned, as I felt a twinge in my shoulder, for the next instant Shian had turned, and now stood gazing down at me with tender solicitude.

Now for the first time I saw, close to mine, that beautiful face which was to dwell in my thoughts ever after.

I saw the face of a woman who was as yet unconscious of her own loveliness. I saw the oval-shaped head with its strong features: enormous, almost black, eyes under long sweeping lashes and dark widely curving eyebrows, a small but perfectly shaped nose, a generous but not too large mouth with well-shaped lips and white, even teeth, and a strong round chin. The whole face was a warm tan color, delicate, yet glowing with vitality.

Slowly, by half opening my eyes for a moment and then shutting them again, I managed to absorb the details of her appearance as her slender body leaned anxiously over me, without alarming her. As she did so her hair slipped forward over her shoulders and covered the young pointed breasts beneath her blue dress.

She answered my weak smile with a look of great tenderness and placed her hand for a second gently on my wound.

"Rest, my prince," she said in soft lilting Irish. "You will be well soon."

It was with difficulty that I hid my wonder at these words. But quickly the significance of her greeting came upon me. I closed my eyes and fell into a reverie. So what O'Hara had said in jest was true! And my wild plan had succeeded. Yet I was uneasy. Had I not at once seen the odd look in Shian's eyes, and guessed that beneath all her tenderness there was that same veil of mystery which had worried Brendan? Here was a woman under a strange spell which denied her the normality of her sex. To say how I knew this so soon would be difficult. Doubtless I was influenced by those webbed fingers, by what I had heard of her wild ways. But sense it I did, immediately, and I wondered how I might break down that barrier between us.

I closed my eyes again, pretending sleep. And soon I heard her sing again.

What a strange song Shian sang—but it was beautiful, too. It haunted me in those long dreams when I lay convalescing on the shore and in the woods. It has haunted me ever since.

When at last I stood up, painfully, Shian led me by the hand to a grassy dais about half-way up the great escarpment. There was a lofty recess in the granite, shaped like a conch shell, airy yet sheltered from the wind and rain. After noon the sun's rays came warmly to the couch of dried ferns and mosses which Shian provided for her prince, Sea-wind, as she now decided to call me.

I came to know and love her well in those hours of tender ministration. I would watch and listen for her every movement and word. In a few days I was able to sit cross-legged in the entrance to our granite bower, basking in the sweet salt air and the rich spring sunlight. She would bring me my food—it consisted chiefly of fish and milk. Some of the fish came from the sea: small flounders, plaice and whiting, perhaps a mackerel; some from fresh water: trout and lamprey and loach. All were young, tender and delicate, melting in the mouth. For I was hungry and ate them raw; and, strangely, I felt no shame or anxiety about this new evidence of my growing animal habits. Later, when I was able to, I gathered some brushwood, rubbed some dry sticks together, and while Shian was away I roasted over a fire some of the young fish. But, finding I preferred them raw, I never again ate cooked food so long as I lived with Shian.

The milk was from the white goats which each evening came to the entrance of our granite hall and awaited Shian. She would milk them swiftly, singing to them an Irish herding song, which they seemed to like to hear. They switched their long white ears attentively. In the night they slept in the grass close by.

A spring of pure water flowed from the roots of royal ferns where the granite joined a slate outcrop. Here I drank and washed.

We were alone, Shian and I. A peaceful happiness such as I had never known closed about us. The sun increased in strength and the wilderness burgeoned with spring flowers. The gulls flew past my ledge, calling incessantly as they began nesting. Cormorants, puffins and other sea-birds occupied the steeper parts of the cliffs, which became murmurous with their excited groans. While the music of the seals mingled at all hours in rhythm with the flow and ebb of the beach waves.

Of man there was no sign, not even the smoke of a hull-down ship, on this forgotten coast. Far at sea were some bird-whitened cliffs, on the edge of the sky—that was all.

In this setting began our companionship. On my side I grew to love Shian for her tenderness and her strength, her grace and her wildness, her wisdom and her naïveté. Her slim body, with its strong limbs and firm young breasts, excited me. But she seemed unawake to her womanhood. Nor, though I am not ill-shaped, but well built, did she seem greatly aware of my manhood, or, if she was, then the knowledge was

61

well hidden. In her frank stare I could only read affection, or, at most, a sisterly love.

Shian, I found, was occupied principally with one problem. To get me well enough to make the sea-journey to the far Holm of the Seals, the theme of her favorite song. I gathered this fact gradually, from the trend of her conversation. At first it was mentioned shyly, as if she was waiting for me to speak first. But as perforce I must hold my tongue because of my throat wound, she became free of hers. I encouraged her with many nods and smiles. I wished to learn her mind so that I could make my plans.

Soon I was glad I was dumb. For I might have blurted out stupid words and scared her with talk of returning to civilization. If I wanted to convey a message I used a chip of granite and wrote with it—in English, the language she could read best—on a flat piece of blue slate. These simple utensils were strewn all over the escarpment. Later, when we were far from these conveniences, I taught her the finger-sign language of the deaf and dumb. She was quick to learn—with many bursts of laughter.

I was determined to wean her from this notion that I was a sea-prince, come to live with her and enjoy her dream of sunlight and happiness amid the lonely rocks on the horizon. But how to begin I could not quite decide. For the moment it was sufficient happiness just to live close to her, while my wound healed. I asked for little else just now—to rest and dream beneath the loving care of this singing child.

Her solicitude clothed me with its tender mantle. Perhaps I pretended to be less well than I was, in order to hold that sympathy longer, in order to put off the day of our absurd voyage, while I thought of excuses which would coax her in the opposite direction? Eventually I would take her back to a civilized life, where a woman of her pedigree and loveliness truly belonged.

Meanwhile it was clear even to Shian that I was unfit for the sea-journey.

"Tell me," I wrote on my slate one day, "what you remember about your early days?" At first she refused.

But I put the slate upon a knob in the cave and would point to it every evening, until at last the story was told. And this in brief is what Shian said:

"I have wanted to tell you of a dream which often comes to me. It is the only remembrance—the only picture that remains with me—of the earliest part of my life. And maybe it was always a dream, but I don't think so, for it keeps coming back to me as if it had really happened, and part of this dream I know to be true."

She stroked my forehead for a moment. This was the only time she would touch me—before talking to me—as if bidding me be at peace. I smiled and took her hands in mine and lightly spread the fingers and touched the webs, which I had grown accustomed to and which even amused me now. But gently she withdrew her hands.

"I dream," she said in her singing voice, "that I am my mother. Is that strange? For I cannot remember her as a living person. Yet I dream I am my mother, and always in that dream I see a field of corn with a strong sea-wind from the west sweeping over it. And this sea-wind is calling my mother. My mother is a shepherdess living on a moorland, inland beyond the corn-fields. But every year when the corn is ripe and the sea-wind blows over it my mother answers the call of this wind and goes down through the corn to the edge of the sea. And there my dream changes and my mother becomes me! I am a very small child lying on the shore in front of the seal caves; and I am playing with the young white seals on the pebbles!"

The next instant she was gone to her sleeping place. Where this was I did not know. She would vanish so swiftly.

Shian could not bear to talk of her grandparents or their house. She would grow silent when I pressed my slate with its request upon her ... When I persisted she suddenly burst into tears—always swift with her, as swift as her joy—and ran from the cave. I gave up trying, but reluctantly, for how else was I to root out the absurd legend, and bring her back to a true realization of the future I was planning?

One day, in a flood of tears, she begged me never to mention them again.

"Sea-wind! All that is past, don't you understand? I would burn that house if I could! It has an evil spirit in it! I would purify it with fire! Granny was put under a spell and died there! Brendan went away, and died . . . We are all under a spell. Only you, Prince Sea-wind, can free us. For you too are under a spell, the spell of a silent tongue, until you join the folk of the sea at the edge of the western sky! Then you will speak aloud again. I know! I am certain!"

She flung her arm toward the sunset. Her face was flushed with a wild emotion. Again she cried out:

"Aren't we all, all of us under a spell? But the future is ours, Sea-wind, and we shall be free—once we have made the journey!"

Her grandmother had told her that the sea-prince's name was Sea-wind, she had said shyly, when asking my permission "to use the name so familiar to me." Hadn't I fulfilled the prophecy by coming to her out of the ocean? By coming to her in glory, having slain that monstrous bull whom she distrusted, that lewd dictator of the folk of the sea?

From the threshold of my granite cottage I saluted with delight the young summer. I was whole at last. I longed for action—to walk and run in the sunlight, to bathe, to feel my stiff muscles loosen again.

That morning I signed to Shian that I would accompany her. I would explore the forest—at first; although she had wanted me to visit the sea.

"Come!"

She pulled my hand, and danced about me. She began a wild chant of joyful boasting nonsense. I tightened my belt about my tattered trousers and felt my knife safely in its sheath.

We climbed to the top of the escarpment, where a storm-cock sang triumphantly from a twisted wind-blown ash with his repeated whistle: "Really, really, really!"

To this his versatile brother the throstle, from a more lowly station, emphatically answered: "De-ar, de-ar, de-ar! No-sleep, no-sleep, no-sleep! Until, until, until! My pretty-comes, my pretty-comes, my-sweet, my-sweet, my-sweet!"

When we approached the woods, they rang with the spring songs of the birds.

Thus it was that, while the humble-bees still hummed impatiently before the unopened trumpets of the honeysuckle, I was initiated by Shian into the life of the wilderness. We were to live a whole summer, more or less, under the trees, in the thickets, by the trout stream . . .

Cunningly I had persuaded her that in the shelter of the forest I would grow strong for the long sea-journey.

Chapter Five

The warmth of summer lay upon Kilcalla.

Each morning Shian came to me smiling, the water of the sea or the brook still glistening in the sun-bleached edges of her dark hair. Often she woke me with a song, with some stanzas describing our adventures of the previous day. Sometimes I slept in the dead leaves under the evergreens, or in a cleft in the rocks, or in the hollow trunk of an ancient beech or oak. I was not particular.

Shian slept alone, but where, I never knew. She would suddenly vanish, like sunlight before a swift-moving cloud, after saying good night. I would turn my head and she would be gone, fled on silent feet into the shadows of the forest. Before this, when I had slept in the granite recess, she had kept watch, as she called it, sleeping in the grass at the entrance while I, still suffering from my wound, lay in warm fern at the back. But as soon as I could walk about she left the cave by night. Once, on a cold evening, I invited her to share its warmth with me, but she laughed and said that we might not sleep together yet, not until the spell was undone, until we got home to the folk of the sea. Then she ran off to some secret niche.

My only anxiety during that most beautiful summer was how to undo the spell which lay upon my companion, to wean her from the sea, back to what men called civilization. But often, in the rapture of living with her in the wilderness, I would forget this problem.

Shian taught me how to survive, care-free, in the wild. She trained me to find delicious food. I learned to eat that which I should have despised a few months ago. Now my strange diet was no longer strange.

She taught me to follow the greater humble-bee to its nest in the mouse-hole. To tear out the mass of cone-shaped cells, sucking them dry of their sweet honey, of their pollen-drowned grubs. Poor creature— you buzz in helpless protest, too dazed and gentle to use your poisoned sword!

When I was weary of eating the delicious wild strawberries which I gobbled down as dessert to my dinner of new-hopping tailed frogs, I would try the juicy young newts which Shian taught me to find under the foam-ringed stones in the low midsummer rills of the woods. For protein I ate the speckled trout, too, and the pink mouthfuls of hairless young from the nests of the mice in the forest litter. The wild clover heads and the thin blades of young woodland grass I would munch as a fill-belly and a tonic.

The natural way of life suited me. I had quickly become a savage, and I gloried in it—at first.

Weather, rain, sun, rock, thorn and water—I no longer felt cold or heat. My body had endured all until now it was attuned and strong. My darkened skin had become proof against the moods of the heavens, the sharp tentacles of the forest, the scratches of mother earth.

My buckskin trousers were little more than a fringe of rags decorating my strong leather belt and sheath knife.

It was high summer. I was full-fed, idle, and, except in my inmost heart, at peace. I pondered upon the exciting multeity of my new home, the forest. I gazed and dreamed.

Once I had learned the trick of swallowing a chestful of air, and of slowly dribbling it forth under water, I found I could stay whole minutes below, searching the stones for the wriggling loach and crayfish. I hunted the woodland pools for black and fallow trout. Sometimes Shian swam with me, or she would sit upon the bank, laughing and singing to me.

Lutra the otter, at first suspicious, had signed a truce with me. She cared not to have me wallowing in and decimating her favorite trout-pools. But she tolerated Shian, and I won her over by my kindness to her cubs. No more jealous or loving mother exists than Lutra. I am excited when I hear her whistle. I love to see her lead her four half-grown puppies through the rapids, or through the water-oak's quiet mirror. I note how well she trains them in swimming, diving and walking. They were poor enough at this last business, and I took it upon myself to give them some lessons in deportment. Once, when one puppy got left a long way behind at the foot of a pebble moraine in the drier part of the river and Lutra searched in panic for him, I picked him up and carried him back to the school under the oak.

For that I was allowed to join in their gambols. Yet Lutra soon grew jealous because the pups found a splendid new game of hide and seek in the water, in and out through my long arms and legs. Secretly, under the water, Lutra gave me a spiteful nip with her ivory fangs. I retaliated with a vigorous twist of her sensitive tail. After that she was more respectful. She realized that I was as quick an aquatic contortionist as she.

In one spot the foxes had recently dug a new earth in the river-bank, and through out a heap of sand toward the water. In the enlarged entrance to the earth I often slept, on warm summer nights. The current had undermined the soft pile, and now it hung, a steep escarpment, over a deep pool. We—Shian, the otters and I—scooped a long groove down this sandy bluff. Then, time and again, one above the other, a living escalator, our warm bodies toboganned downwards into the cool play-pool of the river.

This was pure animal happiness such as I, in civilized days, had never dreamed of. Sometimes, looking up as we played tag with Lutra's puppies after our tumble into the pool, I would see the figure of my new friend, an abandoned fox cub I had fed and cared for with Shian—Dana, the vixen, embossed upon the earth-yellow soil and the blue skyline, one paw raised and ears cocked, as if she were tempted to risk Lutra's dreaded jealousy and join in.

But though I could equal the otters in every gambol, in every exercise under water, I never learned to become a match for Shian, who moved faster even than Flick, the squirrel, in the tops of the trees. I would follow Shian for hours, trying to keep up with her as she leaped through the branches, but always the little figure in the torn blue dress would be ahead, waiting, scolding, laughing at my clumsy progress. I learned to swing from branch to branch with ease, but Shian ever escaped my swift arm reaching out to touch her.

It was early morning.

We stood on the high craggy edge of the Kilcalla wilderness, where it merges by heather and fern upon the foothills of the mountains. Far in the yellow distance a thin plume of smoke told of the nearest human habitation. There were sheep on the slopes ahead of us.

Thus far had I coaxed Shian. Now was the moment to tell her my plans. I pointed to a spring rising from the moss on the green-brown hillside. I spoke by sign language:

"Let us follow that stream."

"But it becomes a river and flows down to villages and towns." Shian knew her country as well as I did.

"It is well you should see a town again." I signed to her with my fingers.

Her huge brown eyes seemed to grow larger. For a moment she was silent. Then she pointed and asked:

"Tell me why we must go down there? For many days now I have noticed you have tried to bring me out of the forest and far inland. What does a prince of the sea know about the folk of the towns? Is it just curiosity, Sea-wind?"

Her look was tender and puzzled.

If only I could explain gently and gradually that I was not of the sea, that I was an ordinary man of the common people who inhabited the land. But words stuck in my throat. My granite and slate writing tools were far away. The gesture language of the dumb was powerless to convey the message burning within me. The sight of house-smoke and flocks of sheep and the feel of the cool mountain wind had suddenly increased my longing for a civilized life. Winter was not so far away, and what would Shian and I do then?

"I belong down there," I signaled at last, pointing to the smoke, and the stream running in its direction. But this she could not understand.

We sat down on a crag edge. Buzzards mewed overhead. Shian's eyes followed them as they soared westwards toward the edge of the forest.

"Look, the big hawks are calling us back!" she said excitedly, and would have risen if I had not held her back.

"Shian, we must talk—a long time," I signed.

"It is nice here," she said restlessly, "but I don't feel safe. Well, what is troubling you, Sea-wind?"

Slowly, painfully, I insisted that I must go down to the towns and meet people. Never mind why (I knew it was useless to explain why), but I must go and I wanted her to come with me. I should protect her from the evil forces she dreaded. I was strong now. If, after we had met people and lived with them for a while, she wished to return to the sea, I would come back with her. I would promise that.

As I spelt out my plea her face became solemn. A look of horror grew in her eyes. She stood up, moving away as she protested.

"Sea-wind, you and I belong to the sea! We must go back there at once! As you are so strong now, couldn't we start our journey to the west tomorrow? They would kill me! They tried to trap me after grandmother died! They hunted me for days and days!"

Her voice rose shrilly, then suddenly stopped. Her look became sad, resigned. Tears again . . .

"Sea-wind," she said, timidly touching my arm, "you go down there if you want to satisfy your longing, your curiosity. If you must go, I shan't stop you . . . A long long time ago I knew villages and towns. You will hate them! To me it was a mystery why people built such places when they could live as we do. There is no peace or happiness there, Sea-wind. Take my advice and stay here. Come, we'll start back."

She ran a few steps westwards and called me. Her voice was normal and happy again, with a singing note in it.

"Sea-wind, Sea-wind! Now! We're going to swim out on our long voyage. I'm ready. Are you coming with me?"

But I turned my head away and stared toward the smoke. To give in now would be fatal. My heart was heavy with dread. What if my plan failed? What if I lost Shian through my clumsiness? Yet the longing for a sight of people, farms, books and civilized things was a deep pain.

I stood up and looked back. Shian's dark head and faded blue dress were visible in the thick heather. She was waiting, hesitating. Perhaps, after all, she would choose to follow me.

I jumped upon the rock and signaled wildly with my arms, pointing eastwards to civilization.

I saw her spring up and take a few steps toward me. Then, as if she was struck by some dreadful thought, the playfulness in her face was gone and I saw a great sadness there.

She came slowly back to me.

"Goodbye, Sea-wind. I will be waiting for you."

She turned, with her head held down, and walked slowly toward the west. The wilderness swallowed her and I was alone, suddenly shivering with the cold in my heart.

Chapter Six

O land of solitude, can I forget
How I have watched a sudden sheet of spray
Leap up triumphant on a stormy day
Above the cliffs, when wintry waves beset
A headland of despair—How I have met
Far inland—wanderers from their native home—
The flying feathers of your ocean foam,
And felt the rushing west wind, salt and wet
With driven mist; But I remember most
How all one night, O melancholy land,
By lone Liscamor bay I could not sleep
For listening to the voices of the deep—
The trampling of a never-ending host
Upon the desolation of the sand.

These lines by Edmond Holmes suited my mood, and ran in my head many times during the long winter, which dragged by like an evil dream. I read volume after volume of poetry in an endeavor to achieve some measure of philosophic calm, as I worked and lived mechanically at the office, and rested at home.

It was of little avail to swear to myself that I would never return to Kilcalla, that I had done with the wayward seal-woman who had rescued me from the sea, then bewitched me with her chaste love, with absurd legends, promises of great happiness among the merfolk. Yet the more I determined to settle to my affairs in London, the more I was unable to resist the desire to abandon my dreary city life and return to Shian.

In this low indecisive state I had fallen ill. Physically I had lost much weight, alarming my sister, so that she called in the doctor without my permission. He insisted that I must rest and avoid excitement . . . otherwise, he hinted, there might be a complete mental breakdown. My long absence and my cadaverous appearance had been remarked upon unfavorably, but I had been spared the difficulty of attempting to explain; my tongue was conveniently inarticulate. Nor did the specialist hold out hope for the recovery of speech in the immediate future. In my present condition he could not operate—my throat was improving, yet the walls of the larynx were still weak. In another year, perhaps . . . I listened impatiently, but perforce in silence.

Not that I had really given up Shian; far from that! As the year turned my spirits and health revived. Carefully I made my plans. But it was some months before I was able to engage and try out a new chief clerk who seemed likely to be competent to manage the business profitably in my absence.

I let it be known that this summer I would be away probably many months. When my sister, concerned at my continuing lean appearance, offered to accompany me, I refused, saying that I intended as usual to rough it, far away from towns and villages. She sighed, saying affectionately: "You're quite hopeless! You're crazy!" Then adding, as she saw me make my simple preparations of packing a satchel with some books, new buckskin trousers and leather belt, with its new sheath holding my old, trusty boyhood knife: "I sometimes think you will never grow up! Take care of yourself all the same."

It was a fine May morning when I reached the Kilcalla wilderness. I discarded the clothes of civilization, and with the satchel over my shoulder, walked barefoot into the forest, joyfully filling my lungs with the pure air scented with spring flowers. Yes, joyfully, for now I had at last returned.

I had every confidence I should find Shian. Had she not promised to be waiting for me? Had I not dreamed of this reunion so often it was already a reality?

When, after five days' eager searching and waiting, I realized she had quite disappeared, no sign, no footprint along the shore or in the damp woodland paths; when I found, too, that her goats were running wild, unmilked, with kids at foot, a new despair overwhelmed me. The sun seemed to go out and the cold shadows of cloud, cliff and forest loomed menacingly closer.

(Fool that I was to think that I had any right to hold her to her promise to wait for me all through the bitter storms of winter on this lonely shore! While I had enjoyed the comfort of my town home, with its cosy warmth and amenities, she had faced alone the terrible gales and hardships of the incessant Atlantic storms—many a night in mid-winter I had been unable to sleep, thinking with dread for her as the wind moaned through the leafless trees outside. Deserter, coward—I had not lifted a finger then to return, to find and protect her!)

Hour after hour, day after day, alone, I continued my vigil. I shivered in the rain, then tried to warm myself when the sun came out. After six days I was worn down with my search, feeling ill again, and desperately needing rest and sleep.

I lay down on the very spot where, a year ago, Shian had tended me. I fell into a dreamless stupor.

On the seventh morning I woke to find Shian by my side.

Shian had been on a long journey. She sang to me the saga of her astonishing voyage. When I did not return after many weeks, she decided to swim to the Holm of the Seals, many miles toward the Skellig Rocks on the western edge of the horizon. This was the resting and moulting refuge of the Atlantic tribe of the Kilcalla herd. She had half expected me to return to her there. Side by side with the mother seals and the last season's calves—the old bulls traveled separately—it had been an exciting voyage. In particular she had made friends with a young cream-colored seal, who had been considerate toward her—a novice on her first crossing. Hali had shown her the wonders of the ocean floor, deep beyond any depth she had yet dared to dive. He was a charming companion, full of games and water-play like all adolescent seals; but of course (she added with what I thought rather smug complacency—or perhaps it was only her naïve warm-hearted trust?) she had dreamed of her Sea-wind, longing for his return from his inland journey to examine the people of the land and towns. How had he fared in those dreadful places?

"Sea-wind, you are ill—but I'm not surprised. I would die in those crowded places they call civilization! How thin you are! But now you will recover quickly." And without waiting for me to tell her the story of my visit to civilization—laboriously with pencil or with sign language—she went on blithely to describe the Holm as a place of many marvels.

It was filled with sea-birds and maritime flowers of vivid beauty. The grass of the Holm was long and pleasant to sleep upon. She had been sad not to have her sea-prince there to share its treasures and explore its reefs and cliffs. But Hali had been a courteous companion, and although he could not leave the sea he had guided her to every cave and underwater grotto, and shown her where best to find sea food. She had been almost happy. When they had rested on the low-water rocks after eating their catch she had talked to Hali of how Sea-wind would return to be their wise prince and protector of the seals, once he had satisfied himself that the life of man upon the land was leading more and more to disaster, war and annihilation. Sea-wind would keep the seal herd intact, and long after man had destroyed the land, the sea would remain—their undisturbed playground.

I listened in deep wonder at this naïve wisdom spouting from the singing lips of my sweetheart of the sea. Her confidence, her faith in me, was warming me through and through. I nodded agreement to her smiling remarks, her impossible fairy tale of how, now that I was safely back, we would make the sea-journey together. We would dwell forever with her people, in the sunlit sea, among the tides and the fishes, in peace and plenty.

I saw a great change in Shian. Her attitude toward me was that of a woman awakening to the significance of male love. She would lean over me at times, and look at me with a new understanding in her splendid eyes. Then she would turn away as if she knew I had gazed—as in truth I had—too ardently at that graceful body, at those firm breasts, now rounder and fuller, which were scarcely hidden by the tatters of the faded blue smock. Her hand was warm with promise as it lay for longer moments in mine.

Transformed with happiness in this evidence of her ripening love, I basked in its magic. My strength returned rapidly, as the sun and sea-wind browned my naked chest, legs, arms. To please her I agreed, without much reasoning (except to consider that if a slender creature like Shian could swim to the Holm of the Seals then I could too) to make the journey to the Skelligs . . . as soon as I felt well enough.

When Shian first saw me nod this affirmation, the light of happy love in my eyes, she suddenly flung her arms about me. And for the first time I kissed her, my lips passionately holding hers. For a moment she responded, then broke away, and ran—embarrassed—into the woods.

When I found her we sat a little apart, shy, but lest I misinterpret her feeling for me she put her hand in mine, pressing it from time to time. And she began her old song, the Song of the Sea, with a wild triumphant cadence, and with new verses added, describing our life together where the merfolk dwell. In the land—or sea—of heart's desire we would be forever united, and all our troubles gone. The spells that lay upon us would vanish. I would no longer be dumb, I should be able to sing again, and she would lose all her fears.

All through the winter an overwhelming loneliness had sickened and devoured me. But now my whole strength and lust for life was upon me as I watched and followed my beloved one.

Never had Shian seemed so beautiful, completely happy and desirous. She was like a child let loose from school. She would run, often singing, through the forest, leading me that familiar game of hide and seek, at which she was so expert. But now it had a new meaning—and ending.

She would step silently behind a tree-bole and lay her slender body flat against the trunk. She would creep under bushes and lie there, hidden, save for those tell-tale toe marks in the moss. When, or if, I failed to find her, she would burst into song, leap up and swing into the tree-tops—always just out of my reach.

Together, while we waited for my complete recovery, and for the day of the herd's departure for the Holm, we watched the procession of the birds and flowers in the forest and along the escarpment.

To my surprise Shian took a deep interest in the books I had brought in my satchel. She spent many a happy hour looking through them. We kept them in a hollow tree, beside our favorite sunlit clearing in the woods, to preserve them from the salt wind.

Often I watched her, in this woodland bower, puzzle over a plucked flower, turning the leaves of the book of the flora. Sometimes in the fine calm days she would leave the flower unidentified upon the page, forgetting perhaps to return that day, diverted by some other joyful occupation.

We would spend half-hours naming a handful of flowers we had gathered. What joy for us to compare the fine colored plates of the book with the exquisite living blossoms! Once or twice I, too, was so absorbed that I did not hear her slip away in her search for a new flower, inspired by its picture in the book. Perhaps when I got back to our hollow tree—our "library" as she called it—I would find the pages of the flora turned to a new place. I would find my herb exchanged for another, asphodel for bistort, bee-orchid for arrowhead, fleabane for tufted vetch. Thus we refreshed our minds with the charming titles, which Shian announced with a flourish of triumph in her sweet voice; dog's mercury, barren strawberry, coltsfoot, wood anemone, dandelion, primrose, lesser celandine, golden saxifrage, marsh marigold, wild hyacinth—these had

77

been the earliest flowers, already in full bloom at the time of my return to Kilcalla.

The second volume was a book of the fauna, newly published. It pictured in color and described the birds and other animals, including the lesser wild creatures such as snakes (none in Ireland), newts, frogs and fresh water fishes. How we laughed at the clumsy portraits of the seals! And the remarks about them: "Habits: very little known. There are many legends . . ."

Shian's joy in our books was such that for a foolish moment I had fresh hope that she might forget her wild plan to leave these, and the other amenities, of the land, and swim far out into the empty cruel sea, to the remote barren Holm of the Seals. Again I pretended to be less well than I was; I remained much in the shelter of the forest, poring over the books while she ran down—far too often—to bathe in the sea, I would try to coax her back to our studies by finding a new flower, or opening the book at the page with the portrait of a new summer bird I wanted her to look at.

For a while she would again be absorbed by the problem of identifying the species. But more and more now I would find she had left the book open, forgotten for a day, or a day and a night, until dew and rain dimmed the printed word. The summer wind might lift a page here and there, carelessly folding it double, or dropping a twig or a moulted leaf between, as if to mark the place for us.

Yet in the still warm days when the fresh murmur of the sea-wind in the trees softened to a zephyr of light airs, and the canopy darkened as the burgeoning leaves shut out the sun, I too could no longer resist the sea. The silence and shifting shadows of the forest bored me. I ran to find Shian by the shore.

There were whole days when we spent the sunlit hours swimming with the seals in the waters of the Cape. It was essential, Shian said, that I should make myself known to the herd, before setting out on our journey with them. So she introduced me to the principal characters—not the old bulls, these were too tire-

78

some, too lazy, too lecherous (at certain times), rather brainless creatures. She was concerned that I should know the matrons (for the gray seal colony is a matriarchy) who really decided the migrations of the herd. Oldest of all was Blind Medrim who, despite her loss of sight, still led the herd by a mixture of cunning, instinct and long experience. One sniff of identification Medrim gave me—a somewhat contemptuous acceptance and greeting I thought—before she rolled her huge bulk back to sleep on the low-water reef.

One day Shian took me to the blue slate pebble beach near where, she said, she had been born. There was a fine long cave at the back of this beach, with a dark echoing recess in its farthest interior—too dark for me to see anything at all. But Shian knew every foot—by touch—as we swam as far as it was possible to go, at high tide, in utter darkness, reaching the birth site. I listened with secret dread there, as she sang the full stanzas of the Song of the Sea. I longed to get out of this eerie stifling hole, into the summer sunlight.

Nevertheless I pretended a deep interest in everything to do with the sea, for only in water was my seal-woman really at home.

It was in river water that our first mating took place.

How describe that wonderful moment adequately? For days she had hovered on the edge of yielding to me. Then it happened, almost casually—as so many events did with this perfectly natural woman. I had called her back to look at a new orchid I had found; and for a moment she stared at the flower, comparing it with the illustration in the book. Then suddenly she tugged me lightly by my blond hair—now grown long—and said with almost a little scream, breathlessly, in her wild excitement:

"Come! It is time . . . Sea-wind!"

Leaving the volumes open upon the mossy altar of our sanctuary she ran singing to the edge of the great pool in the trout stream below. I ran after.

When you peel the bark of the elder a clear ivory stalk is left. Shian's tattered blue dress was the bark from which emerged her ivory torso, supple and perfect, as she deliberately slipped the last rage from her body. Like some rare wild blossom rooted in the moss of the water's edge, long legs and slender hips supported the lean convexity of belly, and above, the firm cups of her breasts, starred with larchbud nipples, and caressed by that wine-dark hair—that glory which of late she had allowed me to plait and play with. Yes, every part of her was perfect—and I deep in love.

For one moment she stood waiting, while her shining black-brown eyes invited me. Suddenly, shyly, mischievously, she stepped close, and unfastened my belt. Then she dived into the pool, shattering the quiet mirror which, for a few surprised seconds of stillness, had reflected the idyll of two forms transfixed with love.

Naked, I plunged headlong. As I swam through the whirling water my left hand caught her heel. I drew her, unresisting at last, toward me. She wriggled easily to face me, and sliding upwards, pressed her breasts against my heart, her arms about my neck. Then I knew a woman's urgent desire freed for the first time.

Tighter and tighter we enfolded. Her eyes were closed on the unuttered confession of her consent. We floated, locked together in the water mating of the merfolk; and its uttermost delights all my manhood strove to know.

The embrace of mated seals lasts long. I remembered that, even as we drifted in the blessed peace of requited passion.

Shian at last floated free. With familiar litheness, she swam in playful pursuit of the luscious trout which had impudently nibbled around our heated bodies. Perhaps this was a diversion, to hide her confusion, her wonder, at her gain—and loss?

The silly fish gaped at the intruders, gamboling in their pool. Swiftly I joined in the hunt. I tickled two large speckled males until my nails could close in their flesh, and brought them ashore.

We ate our fish lunch upon the fallen oak bough, dropping the crumbs to the cannibal brothers of the trout below us.

Laughing softly, invitingly, still perfectly naked,

Shian ran like a deer through the larches. I followed her to the low thicket of sallow, alder and rosebay willowherb, upon a little hilly rise where—she admitted —she had slept apart from me earlier in the summer. Now she revealed this secret hiding place of hers. She lay there, drying her body in the sun, singing her rambling songs. She rested her head in my lap, looked up at my eyes, blushed confusedly, then pretended to sleep while I stroked the ivory of her naked body— ivory only for a little while, until the salt air and heaven's fierce light was to burnish her completely.

At last she slept, and soon drowsiness compelled my tender movements to cease.

In the cool of the evening, she woke first, and turned to kiss me before she went down to the sea. But I would not let her go. I pulled her gently, firmly back into our nest. I compelled her to yield again, though she shook her head and laughingly forbade a land mating—at first, and until I had roused her.

But this seclusion in our woodland happiness was all too brief. Never again was I to lure Shian back to the great dark pines, the golden oaks, the green beeches, the sighing willows, the babbling trout river. She had lost all interest in these; never more was I to hear her sweet voice singing of the flowers and birds, upon the psaltery of the trees. The once beloved books were to moulder in the hollow oak, forgotten forever.

Every day—and all days now—we swam along the edge of the great pebble beach. The seals were gathered and restless, and their musical moans echoed in the tall cliffs.

Chapter Seven

Far ocean, outside the resplendent golden path of the rising sun, had a gray-blue look. Young morning had surprised old sleeping night on the dark edge of the horizon.

Strange-shaped white wisps of cloud sprawled slowly across the roofless blue of the sky, like handfuls of wool blown astray at shearing time.

Behind us in the east, the land looked dark, unfriendly, as yet menacingly shadowed. The sun lit up only the simian thrust, the bright sea-sharpened fangs of the topmost rocks.

Before us the sea beckoned with laughing cones and little pin-pointed waves. I swam through these myriad nipples of the ocean, moving slowly, deliciously forward, the sun warming my naked shoulders. I swam westwards, Shian by my side.

The morning shadows still haunted these little waves of the sea. As they faded, my sleepiness vanished. I smiled upon Shian, and saw the sun kiss the wet fringe of her hair and the white foam of her wake.

Thus we swam forward slowly toward the west, between the white breasts of the tide-races. Now swaying north with the north-going current, now south with the southward stream of the tide, we left the land and felt beneath us the deep breathing of Mother Ocean. Sometimes we rested, our bodies entwined, as we floated together in the long and blessed peace that follows consummation. For in the sea, Shian was ardent, and I was happy, a completed merman at last.

This was the golden hour of my life. I was excited with the new liberty of the sea. Yet it was one of severe physical trial, for I was striving with an element that was harsh and alien . . . in order to please Shian.

She taught me some surprising accomplishments. It was astonishing to find that I could drink and enjoy the sea, like the seal and the sea-bird. My throat improved rapidly. But even salt water, curative and strengthening as it is, cannot dilute the saliva and pacify the workless intestinal fluids of a young and healthy merman.

The sea-swallows, those new friends of mine, which fluttered overhead as I floated in the eddies of the tide-races, are dipping and diving upon a cloud of sand-eels. I open my mouth like the sieve-throated whale. I glide through the translucent water toward the wriggling shoals. Shian follows after me.

But man's tiny mouth is all-adapted for such work. The mischiefs dart away, after wickedly plucking at my long sun-yellowed eyelashes. Another nestles for a second impudently in the shell of my ear. At last I catch one, in the tangle of my blond curls. I swallow it whole.

Ravenously hungry now, I leap forward like the hunting cormorant, arching over and down . . . down and down . . . dribbling bubbles of air from my nostrils as the pressure of the water deflates my chest. I seek bigger game. What shall I find in the rich lumber rooms of the ocean?

A black and white object flashes upwards past me. There is a fishy hint of silver with it. Instantly I turn and shoot after it. Anything will serve me in my desperate hunger.

What, feathers under the water?

It is a sea-parrot, his rainbow bill neatly packed with a row of sprats for his chick in some hole in the cliffs. My long arm outswims him. He is my prisoner as we breach the surface.

Skua, the sea-hawk, was there waiting for him too! No, no, my dear brown-winged friend, not this time!

"Ahr, ahr, ahr!" growls poor Mr. Puffin, dropping his sprats into my open grinning mouth, and trying to pinch my nose with his formidable bill. His needly claws tear my palms. He is absurdly angry and brave, for such a small fellow. Moved by his courage I release him, reluctantly, for his plump little body has made my fingers tingle with a pleasant sensation. Skua darts with a scream of disappointment at the scurrying sea-parrot, who wisely dives under water.

I follow, Shian close behind, evidently pleased with my skill. Soon I am thrashing the chocolate-colored tangle. I part my umber foliage of the laminaria eagerly. Rosy-tinged wrasse with thick green lips gambol clumsily in the ochreous roots. But when I fling myself after them they escape nimbly. They mock me from behind the bars of their submarine retreat, derisively sucking in and spitting out the gritty water with their gaping mouths. They seem to poke their fleshy tongues at me. Shian discreetly withdraws. She does not wish to see me embarrassed.

I struggle to reach them. My face is bruised against the bulbous stems of the oar-weed. As I pause, anxiously wondering if I can snap up one or two of a shoal of whiting which waver like aspen leaves in the light filtered through the laminaria tops, I feel a sharp pinch at the calf of my right leg. I leap, twisting sideways like a scared saithe. My hands grope in the blackness behind me. They catch the long tail of a huge conger, which, alarmed at his audacity, slithers oilily through my fingers, leaving them fouled with a silken slime.

Suddenly our breakfast of whiting, which swam so appetizingly above me, vanishes like winnowed chaff. A shadow has pierced them with a boomerang swiftness. Instantly I crouch flat, pressing the wrack ribbons together to conceal my conspicuous blond body.

It is only Shian, my beautiful mate. Nothing escapes her wide dark eyes. Now she treads water as she stares at me, mocking merriment expressed in the curve of her pursed lips. Her sleek, sinuous body and thighs writhe with controlled power, ready to send her like a torpedo onwards.

I take my hand from the hilt of my knife. I open my fingers, wondering if I too will acquire webs, like those of the tribe of the seals?

Shian dives into the weed-forest and returns instantly with three little whiting, still alive. She nods at me, her water-enlarged eyes blinking encouragement.

Thus we make our breakfast of the bread of the sea together, Shian and I. With a wave of her little arm Shian guides me through the paths of the sea-forest, into the sunlit shallows where the oar-weed grows thickest. I follow close to her gliding body. We float together on the surface of the warm, greenish-yellow water, busily eating the whiting, sucking the honeycomb clusters of the whelk, munching the sweet sea-cucumbers. Warmth and a feeling of well-being return to my once hollow belly.

In the distance we see a small boat with a fishing number upon its bow. Shian holds up a warning hand. With a gleam in her black eyes she rolls backwards, to swim swiftly under water.

The fishermen are hauling lobster-pots. As each one slowly rises on its long rope from the depths of the weed, Shian dives forward and tilts it upside down. If a lobster, crab or crayfish falls out, she snaps it up neatly, careful to avoid the angry claws. Shian works with a smile, with childish glee.

But very few slip out—most of them are still trapped by the wicker-funnel, like squirrels in a wheel-cage.

Now it is my turn to show off. Shian is afraid to be seen near the surface—a naked sea-woman. As the pots rise slowly from the weedy sea-floor I empty them under water one by one, flinging the shell-fish against the stone tied beneath each basket. One blow and they are paralysed. Soon we have gathered a dozen fat lobsters, crayfish and crabs.

We are followed by a swarm of shrimps; they devour the tidbits which are bespattered from the broken carapaces. I leave nothing in the pots except the rubbish of the sea: the goat-eyed squid, the little dogfish shark, the seaweed—draped spider-crab, the poisonous sponge-crab, the crawling sea-lice, the brittlestars and the sea-slugs.

I enjoy the sight of the crocodile-mouthed conger,

the same that bit me, going aloft, mumbling as an old woman, slithering desperately in the wicker cage, its devilish eyes troubled . . . going aloft to be met by the knife of the fishermen splitting its cunning brain in two—for only thus will you kill this sea-cat of the nine lives.

Faintly, as Shian and I carry off our prizes of the willow cradles, we hear the angry groans of the fishermen re-baiting the empty pots—and the flapping noise of the conger's tail beating its death-drum on the bottom strakes of the little boat . . .

Up there, they are moving to new fishing grounds. The bronze propeller kicks up a pretty fountain of swirling bubbles above us. I shoot up for a mouthful of air-snorting with only my nose above the surface, at a safe distance. The fishermen see me—indistinctly. They hurl oaths, at the same time reaching for their shotgun.

"The accursed seals! No wonder we did so badly!"

They have mistaken me for a seal! I drop like a heavy pebble to Shian's side, laughing as best I may under water.

It is strange, but I seem to need little air these days. I gasp a few times at the surface, and these gulps last me long minutes under the water. I lie lazily on my back, in a couch of weed, replete, deliciously full, the skin over my stomach drum-tight at last. I see little luminescent pin-points quivering, darting in the garden of the sea around me, stalked eyes of prawns waiting permission to clear our littered breakfast table.

Above, the beat of the engine is a monotonous symphony echoing in the hull of the little fishing boat. It is accompanied by the silver notes of the gurgling bow-wash, tapping of a thousand fairy hammers riveting her stem. This is the itinerant orchestra of our submarine restaurant. Shian smiles happily at me. As long as we have the fishermen, her nod seems to say, we shall not starve—even if they do!

One moment I am blinking my drowsy lids at Shian in a full-fed sleepy response to her grimace. Then in the space of a nod she has vanished. Shian? Shian?

Imp of the underwater world, where are you? In the second of a heartbeat I am alone and desolate.

Soon I see her hair floating amid the fucus—swiftly to vanish again. The weed swirls like a cornfield in the wind. Next moment I have accepted the invitation. Placing my arms against my sides I lash my thighs. My legs become coiled springs. I shoot head first in the quivering wake of my mate.

In the heat of noon we lift ourselves out with sighs of satisfaction upon the lonely Lemon Reef, heaving our salt-brown bodies upon the wind-dried bladder-wrack. We relax in the golden sunshine, limbs spread to the healing warmth.

The little waves play with my toes; then with a last kiss retreat, to continue their games in the shadowed fissures and caves twenty feet below us. The tide drops far here.

While we sleep, full-fed and dreamless, the sea-magpie, standing on one carmine leg on the highest rock behind us, is our concierge. He sleeps, too, but with one eye open for danger. Otherwise we have the rock to ourselves, Shian and I.

When the returning tide greedily bathes my toes again, I wake with a delicious sensation of warmth and homeliness, so snug, so hot, am I . . . I am reluctant to open my eyes, which have been burnt under their lids by the joint fire of sun and salt. I turn for a game with Shian, my dear sprite of the sea.

Instantly the body beside me draws a heavy protecting flipper over me, encouraging me to nestle closer. Why, it is Medrim, the blind grandmother seal who, last autumn, lost her yellow calf in the big storm. Now she is trying to adopt me!

There is more than a hint of annoyance in the dumb laugh I give. To be mistaken for a foundling seal—I, a full-blown merman, six feet in my naked toes! What impudence! No matter if Medrim *is* blind and the biggest Atlantic cow on the coast, she should know better than to insult me!

The infamy is made worse by the fact that there are dozens of seals basking around me. They have landed, one by one, while I have lain in my full-bellied stupor. I can see Shian chuckling at me from a distant rock. Her hair shines with salt. She has just come from the tide. She sits close to a young cream-colored bull lolling there. Hali, too, is grinning.

All eyes are turned on me . . .

My strangled snort of annoyance Medrim mistakes for the human wail of her lost calf. She pushes her great body closer, proffering her furry stomach, its old breasts tight with stale milk. The other seals break out with moans of approving laughter, or so—in my fury—it seems to me.

For a moment I look with savage hate into Medrim's opaque unseeing eyes. Then in my passion I rise steadily to my feet. I will show them that I cannot be counted a mere seal after all! Can the seal balance upright—on his weak, webbed hind flippers? Can even a fine cream-colored bull seal open his legs and stride across the rough rocks?

I do both, smiling triumphantly.

At once the watchful sea-pie rises with a loud pipe of warning. He screams:

"Man, man, man!"

One startled look at me and the seal herd plunges headlong into the laced flounces of the sea. Even blind Medrim rolls into the depths, infected by the panic. And Shian too vanishes—with her friend Hali.

I am left suddenly and completely alone.

Dark heads re-appear in the surf, making a circle around the dwindling pinnacle of the Lemon Reef. They gaze at the human pillar—this dreaded figure of MAN. There is fear and questioning in their huge shining eyes. My anger vanishes in my overwhelming dread of loneliness.

I hold up my arms in dumb appeal. But I only alarm them more. There is a simultaneous loud splash. Rings of foam appear in place of brown snouts. The herd has moved off, under water, into the deep.

I leap into the widening saucer of foam where last I saw Shian. Torn with anxiety I thread the empty depths in pursuit.

Shian, where are you, my golden-coated love? Have you forgotten me already?

When at long last I shoot upwards, foiled in my search and gasping for breath, I pass through a stratum of sepia. I breach the ceiling of the sea, to find it grown dark and quivering. Above, the sun is twice its normal size, dilated by the hoary breath of the coming storm. There is a gray halo around it, accentuating the unreal light.

A hissing wall of water is galloping toward me from the west.

Shian, darling sweetheart of the wave, how may a poor novice weather the storm without your guidance?

I am forsaken in the cradle of the immense ocean. Yes, I could even lay my head on Medrim's old stomach now, in my agony at Shian's elopement.

I look around fearfully at the gathering blackness of the storm. No human or seal head anywhere. I stumble at the edge of the sea. I fall, downwards through the indigo water. Gathering speed, my listless body hurls silently down, I care not how deep. Since now I have nothing to live for, let me sink downwards to darkness, to the compressed ocean slime, the burial ground of the sea.

I was carried deep by the avalanche of my swift despair when I sank, obedient to the force of gravity, a ship's lead snipped from a heaving-line. I thought I should sink and sink, until the black deep forever swallowed me, in an icy suicide; but my shoulders suddenly struck the shelly marl of the sea-floor. There was a sounding blow on my back and the sand whirled through my trailing hair.

There, at the bottom of the sea, safe from the pounding of the hurricane, I found her.

Shian was waiting for me after all, the playful imp. She had been amused by the whole incident. One mischievous look she gave and a smile seemed to hover in the corners of her red lips. Her face was smooth and tranquil as she shut her eyes in a snatch of sleep.

In the underwater twilight her body glowed as with a

yellow fire. Her hair was loose, straying amid the heavy fingers of the laminaria. A few wisps floated in the current set up by my treadwater movements, to blind my seeking eyes and mingle with my own blond hair. And now I needed air. But she remained perfectly still, cradled in a couch of weed-lined rock, her hands folded in her lap, her head thrown slightly back.

In a little while however her eyes opened. She took my hand reassuringly. Together we rose to breathe deeply at the surface; then settled to sleep in a warm tidal niche in the rocks of the Lemon Reef.

Shian slept all through the night and the storm, confident in the protection of my arms. I too slept, but uneasily, for my inward fears turned into strange dreams, once more no trouble me. In one dream I drifted with Shian in the blue-green savannahs of the sea. Hand in hand we explored the seven meadows of the ocean. We climbed the blue icebergs of the north. We swam in the coral lagoons of the south. Eagerly I showed her a thousand watery treasures of the ocean.

In another dream, storms tossed the gray surface. We sank below to a chill dark calm, a grave of the sea. I crouched at her feet, chafing her frozen limbs in my cold palms, on the floor of the Atlantic. It was hard to see through the gloom, but the deep sea held dread dangers. I was afraid—but of what?

Often a man will wake of a night, beset with nameless foreboding, having experienced a fearful nightmare. Half conscious in the twilight of a dream, he longs for the light to come. In my dream that night I could sense a dangerous presence drawing near.

A slender garfish, boring its blind path, follows its spike-nose until it collides with Shian's brown shoulder. With one sweep of my arm I have the eelish dolt. My long nails pierce its slimy scales. I fling it to the greedy crayfish, carrion-scavengers of the depths, which all this while have been waiting in the shrubbery around me—only their long red and yellow whips have been visible, quivering in hungry anticipation.

But as they rush forward to feast, a giant dogfish, little less than a man-eating shark, rolls past, making one drunken downward lurch with his sharp snout, sucking in the iridescent, dying garfish. Bluish-gray shadows behind me swallow him, while the spiny lobsters, clicking the bases of their reticulated antennae angrily, shoot backwards into retreat.

At that moment, vivid terror in my heart, I turned to find a huge brown shape menacing us. It had come upon us silently in the black depths of the night sea.

At first I saw the horrible mouth open, showing rows and rows of saw-like fangs. Fear and rage possessed me as my hand grasped my knife. I thrust forward with a slashing movement of my arm. In one demi-second the sharp blade had run sweeping the full length of the encrusted shagreen of the stupid sea-wolf. I struck with a strength that surprised both of us, at the same time thrusting Shian aside with my other arm.

I felt the fat blubber rushing apart, like jelly under my splendid blade. Blood and entrails suddenly enveloped us.

The dying monster threshed feebly downward. The spiny lobsters will undertake all necessary obsequies.

Then it was that a cold wave rolled over me and woke us. I shivered. The tide was rising. Those horrible dreams! Shian was still drowsy, quite undisturbed by tides or night-mares. She nestled against me, the long chains of her hair about my shoulders caressingly. She relaxed in deep sleep once more, trusting my arms.

But I dared not sleep—and dream again. Once more I longed for the sun to rise.

Chapter Eight

A low sweet warble trembled in the gateway of my consciousness. Tired with my night vigil, I rested, half-asleep, in the sunlight at the top of the reef. I feared to lift my lids, lest Shian, whose tiny hand still lay in mine, should know that I was listening. Then she might stop her song.

Many times had I heard that sweet psalm before from the lips of Shian in our rendezvous in the forest.

I hear, too, other songs, not only Shian's. There are seals around us—they are practicing their little scales to the lapping of the tide in the rocks. Theirs is a confused harmony.

Shian turned to smile upon me, as I rose on my elbows to stare with delight upon her warm bronzed face, upon her body, sun-kissed and silky.

We resumed our journey. We swam and drifted all morning upon the tide's breast.

There was change in the color and movement of the water. Silver eddies drew their swift furrows around us in a new quadrille of the currents.

The sea turned to pale lavender, a sheet of oiled silk under the high sunshine. Overhead the sky was a hollow dome of steel blue, not a cumulus wisp to throw a purple shadow upon the sun-burnished water.

We drift, Shian and I; we drift faster and faster, as the ocean current seizes us. We drift toward the violent tide-races which surround the lonely rocks of the western sea. We are drawn into the maelstrom surrounding Little Skellig, the Holm of the Seals.

The shield blisters and splits. A white cliff towers nearer, racing to meet us, a wall blanched by the mutings of innumerable nesting sea-birds. A thousand huge-winged gannets hover overhead, their plumbeous sword-bills pointed, their fish-blue eyes focused down upon us.

We stare in wonder at the molten yellow of these beautiful regimented heads, at the sight of those snow-white plumes, those royal arched fan-tails, those rich black wing-tips splayed wide to hold poised those streamlined silvery torpedoes of the sky!

The gannets dive, as at a given signal. A shoal of mackerel has honeycombed the surface, their white-ringed frog-eyes for one blink showing above water, flashing patterns of opal, emerald and garnet. Too late they shoot into the green depths. The plumes of a thousand fountains spray our sun-scorched faces.

The white arrows dither down, far down, beneath us, then rocket to the light again, each gasping down a mackerel in its grinning bill. One rises so near that its startled squid eyes squint through the quivering arc of Shián's hair. In terror it thrashes forward, trying to free itself. The thick coils entwine its wing-tendons, and Shian is towed backwards into the heaping overfalls of the tide-race. Gannet, Shian, and I in pursuit, dive deep . . .

In the current, in the flooded shallows, I seize and free foolish Sula, the mackerel-fisher. As I comb the disordered hair of my loved one along comes Hali, the adolescent bull seal whose manner is still obsequious. He accompanies us to the sun-baked shore, piloting us to a deep pool in the ochre rocks of the island harbor. But my tender looks toward Shian seem to displease him, for, with an abrupt wave of his flipper, he refuses her invitation to join us. He swims off to his basking place on the reef. I believe that he is jealous that I seem to possess this richly maned princess of the sea.

We climbed up through the burning radii of sun upon rock, up and up until we reached the low plateau of the island.

All around rose the hot dome of the sky, a vivid pipkin of rarest blue. To the west no other world was in sight, no hint of man-infected land, only a faint smudge vanishing—this might equally have been a cloud or the smoke of a hull-down ship. The island's center was a smooth tureen of grass, so emerald that it stung sharply eyes long attuned to the plue palette of the ocean.

Shian came to my arms . . .

Suddenly she laughed. She ran to the edge of the cliff. One hundred feet below, the sea was an ermine-lined cloak of slate-blue, star-spangled with the constellations of the flying gannets.

She flung up her arms. With a mocking glance at me she leaped outwards . . .

Soon I too learned to forget fear, gliding through the air, a swallow, a feather in the sea-zephyrs updrawn by the heat radiated from the white cliffs. The resilient strength of my parabolic leap carried me far clear of the little toes of the cliff peeping so wickedly beneath in the wash of the currents. I could have caught the scattering sea-birds in each hand and carried them downward to the blue water. I hiss past them, their wings buffeted by the wind of my swift flight. A bird of the air at last!

Falling, falling, falling, a light in my eyes, glee in my rosy cheeks, a glad cry on my dumb lips! The long dives of my boyhood are as nothing to these flights!

Soon I have learned to loop in long curves, turning over thrice, delighted with the new sensation, anxious that the rushing windage shall cool every hair of my golden skin. Then as the sea leaps to meet me I straighten for a dive, making a narrow angle.

In, out! Sometimes I leap clear of the water as I rise again, like the rutting porpoise, my momentum fifty times that of the seals. My friend Hali stares at me in amazement from his wrack couch. I glide to a finish, braking with spread arms and chest, to the inner pool of the harbor, the following wave of my wake a shroud rushing with a warm kiss against my air-cooled temples.

The little tempest of my arrival sprays Shian, and laps her sun-burned webbed toes, as she waits at the edge of the sea.

Chapter Nine

For two months we were settled in our warm green la-
masery of the Holm, waiting for the moment when the
summer assembly of the seals would once more begin
to disperse—on those mysterious migrations which as
yet I did not fully understand. Shian and I were complete and happy—most of the time.

Yet, of late I must admit certain fears have returned
to me; and well, yes, the possibility of boredom.

When we first started our island life there was a
madrigal of joy in my heart. Its beauty was so perfect,
so marvelous—shared in the fullness of our union,
body—and soul. I could not want anything more satis-
fying, far from all taint of the mainland way of life.

But the summer was drawing to a close, and as
Shian seemed daily to change and show an increasing
degree of coolness toward my love-making, I began to
wonder what would happen in the coming winter
months. Would she ever weary of the monotony of the
sea and its storms? Would she at last consent to return,
as my wife at last, to the pleasures and comforts of my
home far away in London—those amenities which of
late I thought of increasingly, especially now that the
weather was changeable and cool?

It seemed to me, however, that instead of tiring of
the life, she was turning more and more to the company of the seals, and avoiding me. Each morning she
would lie on the basking rock, talking with the seals in
their own musical moaning language. Being dumb I
could take no part in these intimate conversations, even
had I understood them. Therefore, so is man made,
being neglected, I became jealous—and bored.

Alone, I hunted until I had taken tribute of every edible item in the inventory of the sea and shore, so that in other ways I might please Shian and show my ability as a merman and husband. I sought in every nook of the tall cliffs until I knew the island architecture by heart, each shelf and ledge loaded with the hummock-nests of the gannets, each niche and cornice holding the squabbling loomeries of the guillemots, each fortalice of the growling razorbills, each bracket and fingerhold of the kittiwakes. From all I had levied toll of new-laid eggs. Even Mother Carey's chickens, the dusky white-rumped petrels of the topmost talus, yielded with protesting purr their brown-ringed ivory marbles to me—the last eggs of summer.

Now that the sea-birds had hatched, I collected their fat squabs, deliciously tender to eat, especially those of Sula the gannet, who would point her dangerous halberd at me angrily as I slipped warily past her along the viscid ledges. Sweet Swhee, the black-capped sea-swallow, I also knew—him I would sometimes feed on surplus sprats, him and his piebald downy chicks. I mapped the island with my foot-paths, moving through the bedlam legions of these winged children of the sea. In a short time I grew to know their voices and habits.

Once or twice the scarcements and slopes—for I was growing overbold as a rock climber—betrayed me. My clutching nails filled with the slimy isinglass of the birds' mutings, I would carelessly slip into space. One kick of my powerful feet against the fulcrum of the rock, and I was winnowing outwards and downwards, swallow-diving on a long plane to the sea. Each morning too I perfected my little flights among my friends the sea-birds, as I dived to my daily bath in the clean scour of the currents.

Washed of the excretings of my friends, I continued under the violet surface in my long dive. There in my submarine garden I gathered the little shell fruits: the seedling oysters, the razor-spoots, the delicate thin-shelled clams, sea-helix, the pleated squirt, the lead-blue mussle, all feeders on the fine nektron of the underwater-world, fit food for my beloved. I dug my long fingers in the sand in search of cockles. I picked over the weed at low water in my hunt for the coralline periwinkle.

All these I carried aloft to our eyrie, in a grass basket which I had woven and tied to my belt in an idle moment when lying at Shian's feet. Many times did I fill for her this basket, until it overflowed with the tender carrigeen and laver sea-weeds, on which I love to browse myself when exploring the rocks at low tide.

There was no doubt about it, I thought, now, our honeymoon is ended. The seals are winning Shian over by degrees. She spent more hours among them, talking to them, or sleeping on the same rock by day. I ought not to be jealous because—I noticed—she now neglected Hali. She sought instead the company of the young female seals. She returned only at night to our grass nest, to greet me briefly, and then to sleep. She was no longer ardent for my passionate love.

I was disheartened, even angry at this coolness. But I tried to hide my chagrin.

One morning I ran to the cliffs and made my wild leap. As I floated down through the wheel of the sea-bird flights, I seized in each hand a sea-parrot, bringing their grotesque clown heads together in death-clap.

I raced through the water beneath, closing my talons on the fattest of the golden pollack, on the grossest of the orpulent wrasse.

While the seals rested, I was restless. All day Shian talked to them, while I wasted my energies in jealous fears. She seemed unreasonably placid, lazy, contented. She continued to prefer sleep to my love. Physically frustrated now, I could not sleep.

That evening, before the sun set, Shian turned back on her way to our nest, saying she had to speak with old Medrim, the blind matron. Looking to the east, I saw the porpoise herd move in formation through the shadows of the tide-race of the Holm with simultaneous piston-blows of air from breathing holes in the top of their dusky heads. Hiding my brooding anger at Shian's indifference, I accompanied her back to the sea.

I dived deep, cunningly seeking a fat suckling from the school of cetacean visitors. I bounced upwards, with all my strength driving my knife above the hilt into a young blubber-covered jugular. Thus my anger and bitterness were momentarily relieved.

Leaving the blade fixed I dragged the quivering body toward the rocks. The angry adult porpoises pursued me, whistling their horror in concert. But they were helpless to come ashore.

Out on the land I withdrew the knife, letting the rich blood fill a broad clam shell. The seals watched me with apprehensive eyes. No matter, I was growing desperate.

In the green crater that night, I placed my crimson spoil at Shian's feet. She had arrived very late, and I saw no welcoming smile. When I cut a portion of the thick congealed blood for her, she—whose appetite had hitherto been large and ominvorous—refused it. Her brown eyes were full of reproach and tears as she stared at me.

"Was it necessary to kill a harmless child of the lesser sea-folk?" she asked coldly, and moved away from me.

That evening I could not rest. When the moon rose, I walked despairingly to the sea. I dragged the baby porpoise's corpse to where the currents would sweep it away. Then I swam for hours in the metallic sheen of moonlight, thoughtfully catching in my fingers a dishful of spawning silver fry. Early in the morning I came home, and spread them before Shian, upon a sorrel leaf. Then, weary with my hard chase, I fell asleep at her feet.

When I awoke they were gone. I gazed eagerly at Shian. I saw that she was still asleep.

Then I heard Larus, the great gull, give a satisfied belch. He was swallowing down the last tidbit. Moreover, the clam of congealed porpoise blood had been picked clean, the pollack and wrasse had disappeared, and a few scattered shells spoke of a completed first course. The sea-parrots were nothing but inverted skins.

Next day Shian came to me, saying:

"Sea-wind, don't you understand the sea-folk need much sleep at this season, until the annual moult is completed? We must rest for a month. Then it is necessary for the cow seals to leave the bulls, and make a special journey—alone . . ."

But I could not sleep. Nor could I bear my tormented thoughts in idleness.

I built a little house of driftwood and stones and turfs, open to the south and the sun. I would have coaxed Shian to spend her days of waiting there, rather than with the seals. But she told me that she was afraid to miss the moment when the cows would move off. She began to sleep on the rocks, and would no longer return at night to the igloo.

I took no pleasure in completing it. Yet I must do something, and busy hands helped to avoid bitter thoughts. So I went on with the island shelter, dreaming my vain dream, growing more and more lonely and fearful of the future. Slowly my house grew, and with it—as my sole amusement—my garden.

I took to herborizing in every sheltered nook of our green cradle in the Holm of the Seals. I made a border of fig-marigolds, tapestry for our palliasse of sun-dried holcus blades. The mesembryanthemum can live without roots in that salt air. I painted the stones of our bed-chamber with yellow and silver lichens, and in every joint between them I tucked the roots of sea-campion, lady's fingers, corniculatus, matricaria, saxifrage and armeria.

There was a strange plant I could not name, a kind of orchid with curious gyrose petals, yellow and crimson—not unlike the mimulus but with a scent of spikenard. In the evening it radiated a golden light, as if luminescent, and filled the nostrils with a sweet aromatic, even narcotic, fragrance. It never seemed to fade, but would lose its flexile touch and assume the wax-like smoothness of the stephanotis.

It was with this unnamed flower that I had made a wreath, to crown my Shian's hair, on the day after we landed, so that the prophecy she had made in the later stanzas of her Song of the Sea might be fulfilled.

All her prophesies were being fulfilled, one by one. Now and then she would look anxiously at me, saying:

"Speak, Sea-wind, surely you can speak to me now that we are safe and secure in our true home?"

But I was silent, as ever—save for a cough, or a grunt. And now each day I had become even more morose and reserved. The truth is I was deeply unhappy, jealous that Shian had turned completely to the seals for company. I had little wish to speak now.

One evening, while she rested sleepily with the group of young mated females which conversed in their sing-song moans on a rock, apart from the male seals, I crept silently toward her, and concealing myself in the cleft above, watched her for a long time, trying to understand this baffling mysterious mate of mine. I saw her smile at intervals as she slept; and I knew that I loved her more deeply than ever. Whatever happened I would stifle my ungenerous thoughts, and follow her, even if I were drowned in the wilderness of ocean . . . If only I could really and fully become an animal, an unthinking seal man!

The sun turned blood-red. As the gray loom of night besieged the eastern sky, the clamor of the roosting sea-birds was stilled. Most of the fledglings had already abandoned the cliffs for their true home, the boundless ocean. Soon the Holm would be quite deserted of their friendly cries and whirring wings.

It was cold. Reluctantly I returned to my lonely bed in the igloo. Afar off, in the rocks a hundred feet below, I heard the seals awakening. Lately they had commenced a strange kind of evensong. Tonight their vespers were unusually prolonged.

Chapter Ten

By the morning Shian had slipped away. After a long search I could not find her. Nor was there a cow seal left on the reefs.

The females had moved in the night, and Shian had gone with them. Again I searched the island, and waited all day long, but in vain. Only the bull seals were present, sluggishly sleeping.

It was a wild evening when I gave up the search and turned back to my island hut, my heart aching. Ahead of me to the south a great storm gathered with terrifying darkness. Soon a demoniacal roar began as the sea battered the rocks below. In the northern sky the shafts of the autumnal aurora played in a prismatic dance with the stars. But the male seals lounged lazily in the heavy surf as if nothing was worrying them, when the full tide swept the basking rocks.

At the door of the igloo Larus, the great black-backed gull, stood at his accustomed sentinel duty. Often have I fed Larus. He has become tame and friendly, my sole company now.

A voice within me was whispering: it warned me that I had better return at once to civilization before it was too late, before winter destroyed me.

Two days later, when the gale eased, I turned my back upon the Holm of the Seals. My empty heart still cried out for Shian. Far in the east the air was stark and clear. Plainly I could see the mountains of Ireland—the coast was ten miles away, the Lemon Reef a black scar halfway.

The tide was full, the current rushing east toward the land. I threw up my arms and dived outwards and downwards upon the upswell of the wind. I swam with long strokes, warmth trickling back into my chilled limbs. I journeyed, a wriggling protoplasm in the hoop-cell of the sea. I was returning to the land. I was going home for good . . . The whole mad sea-adventure was over.

Above me, as I ploughed the watery desert of the Atlantic, the rising sun caressed my brown shoulders with tingling heat. There were restful moments when I rolled over and floated, flat upon my back, under the energizing light.

At times Larus came up to me, as if curious where I was bound; at noon he made a breastsummer of his broad wings and swung his shadow to shield my burning face.

The west wind and the current carried me toward the Lemon Reef. But though I swam eagerly, even angrily, I could not catch up with the cow seals. The sea was utterly empty and cold. If only I had had Shian, a voyager by my side!

I could feel the cruel indifference of the ocean beneath me, in the long impersonal lift and fall of the infinite parallels of the Atlantic swell. I was desperately weary when at last I reached the Lemon Reef.

The sky smoked with violet patches between the torn gray walls of billowing clouds. Before the rose of dawn had left their tattered edges, I was far eastwards of the Lemon Reef. As I swam I reflected on the hopes of the journey, wondering if perhaps, after all, Shian was waiting for me on the Kilcalla Strand? Where else had she gone with the cow herd? There was no doubt that a strange numbness had weakened my mind all through our recent estrangement and I had not yet recovered the power of reasoned thought. The cruel and harsh environment had destroyed my normal philosophic calm and my heart was full of foreboding.

Toward dusk, the white back of a breaking surf carried me far up the pebbles of the familiar bay. I rolled over eagerly, and walked quickly the length of the deserted Kilcalla Strand.

I could not find Shian. Not a sign, not a footprint anywhere.

I climbed to our eyrie in the granite outcrop, and slept the sleep of utter exhaustion. I woke later, shivering, alone.

Days later, after vain searching, I resisted no longer the autumnal gales. They drove me back to civilization.

Chapter Eleven

In the winter I endeavored to forget the astonishing adventures of last summer. But gradually there was a surprising development. I found myself uttering audible, intelligible words. In a few weeks, with a little practice, I regained the power of coherent speech in full.

It was of course a coincidence, but exactly as Shian had foretold, the "spell" of silence laid on me had been lifted—once I had completed the ordeal of the difficult journey to and from the Holm of the Seals. But although I could now talk freely again I did not describe those adventures in the west to a soul. For I had determined to put the whole affair aside for the present, and devote myself to retrieving the family business, which was not thriving as a result of my long neglect.

Despite my efficient head clerk, things had gone badly, with debts piled up; ingratiatingly the obsequious fellow said it had been a slump summer. It was not his fault, he apologized ... I was forced to work hard, burying myself in the accounts, attending to our clients, with whom I could now converse normally. Immersed in business each day, I tried to forget my seal-woman, and in the evenings visited my club, or took my sister to the theater, opera, ballet. To keep fit I played squash in the local gymnasium.

But all the while a certain music resounded in my ears—a sea-song. I found my existence had, after all, a compelling driving force. Shian had never ceased to call ... away there in the far stormy west. In the cold winter nights while the gales blew I lay awake, fearing that my seal-wife was in trouble, in vain trying to convince myself that she was happy with the herd she had forsaken me for; and that she was not desperately lonely, like her human lover.

That song of hers—the Song of the Sea—still echoed in my brain; the seductive music grew louder and louder with the approach of spring.

Yet it was mid-summer before my business was sound enough to leave again, and I was able to announce that I would be taking a holiday. But I gave no firm date for my return—how could I possibly know?

On the next evening I fould myself on my way to the west of Ireland, dreaming that I would surprise Shian with my new power of conversation, even of singing! If only I could find her quickly . . .

That dream was abruptly ended when I found a broad cordwood track cut through the Kilcalla forest to the very edge of the cliffs, where the old slate quarry had been re-opened. A modern crawler-tracter was smashing its way through the woods, drawing rubble to lay access roads through the estate. Men were everywhere, it seemed to me, chopping down trees, blasting rock faces.

It was from an Irish quarryman that I got the harsh facts. This was now the O'Malley Estate Quarries Limited, named from the people who once owned all the land here. Iolo Rees was the manager, an enterprising Welshman from the slate district of North Wales, who had formed a company and leased the whole estate from the Public Trustee—no Irishman would have dared to do such a thing. But Rees was smart, business-like, and knew his job well. Yes, said my informant, they would be felling all the ripe timber of Kilcalla forest. Rees had brought a lot of employment into the district, quite like the good time his grandfather remembered under the old O'Malley squires.

Shian O'Malley? No, she had never come back to the old home—she had disappeared years ago, some people said she was married and in America, like many another Irish lass. But some there were who said she still lived hereabouts, perhaps up in one of the deserted mountain cabins? But that was rumor, like the gossip about Kilcalla House being haunted. The old Baliff O'Hara had died, and the estate was in the hands of the Public Trustee since no one seemed to claim it—there were no direct heirs. Surely I had seen it in the papers—that the famous white cattle had been bought, as a herd, for some nobleman's park? That soon after O'Hara's death the farmhouse had been burned down? It was thought to be a case of arson ... as no one was living there at the time.

I took the new cordwood path toward the lumber camp which he said lay near the remains of the old house. But once out of sight I turned back toward the shore, hearing the ringing of axe and maul grow faint as the murmur of the sea increased. I crawled through the dense thickets of slow and furze which bedeck the steep slope of the escarpment itself, until only the sounds of the birds and the sea-wind filled my ears. Thank God, this part of the wilderness was never likely to be touched by man. I had long ago learned its secret paths, made by badger, fox, deer and gone-wild goat.

My sadness for Kilcalla's ordeal was as nothing beside my longing to find my beloved. Ignoring the sharp thorns which tore my clothes I descended eagerly toward the caves of the seals.

Here, as a last resort, a safe hiding place during the day, I might find Shian, my sea-wife? Unless she had once more swum to the Holm of the Seals?

In a golden couch of the whorled sea-broom I rested, plucking the long thorns from limbs grown tender with soft living. For a moment, out of breath, I basked in the heat of the early autumn sun, looking down into the quivering blue pools and purple deeps of the caves two hundred feet below. It was low tide; I could see only the long wands of the laminaria swaying on the pulse of the sea, below the sun-warmed pebbles. Gulls floated lazily on the updraughts of quiet zephyrs, with mocking calls warning me of the futility of my search—or so it seemed to me.

The strand was quite empty.

Climbing along the lowermost ledges I stared down into each cave longingly. In a moment I would slidedown and plunge into a deep entrance, and continue my search by water. Already my lips formed the one word "Shian!" Ready and poised, it was yet only a whisper, for I remembered she had never heard me utter her name . . . for that matter would not be able to recognize my voice!

Twelve caves lie in a chain on the western end of the strand, guarded by the bastions of granite cliff there. I hid my traveling clothes, and, wearing only my buckskin shorts, belt and sheath knife, I dived into a sun-warmed sea pool. The green-blue water soothed my body after the harsh scratching of the escarpment. I floated to the surface, blowing my lungs vigorously. Swiftly I swam from one cave to another.

Nothing at all, not even a young seal in sight.

Only the outermost caves, facing the full swell from the Atlantic, were left now. Difficult to enter on foot, except at lowest tide, some of these caves I had never fully examined. They ran far up into the land, into the utter darkness—like the cave in which Shian had said she had been born, and which she had shown me; its echoing blackness had secretly horrified me.

I swam through the marbled porphyry of the current swirling around the headland. A languid but powerful swell rocked me as I moved through the confusion of the low-water reefs. The entrance to Shian's cave came slowly into view, its sun-whitened apron of pebbles dazzling to the eye.

At first I could see nothing but the misted dancing of the heated air above the neat terraces of pebbles formed by the succession of the neap tides in fine calm days. At first I could hear nothing but the clap of each wave, as it filtered through the outer rocks and poured beachwards, and paused before there came the rattle of its retreat bubbling amid the smooth slate stones.

Then a wild pounding of my blood began, as in the momentary silence of a spent wave I heard, beyond doubt, the music of Shian's treble voice.

A snatch of words came, blurred but familiar, as I floated atop the shoreward swell:

107

In the wild bay the seals are diving for fishes,
The young calves are playing in the warmth of
   the shallows
As the tide creeps . . .

Then the wave flung itself, as if in furious applause, toward the beach, leaving me sunk in the following trough.

I waited until the next swell carried me in its crest and, as I rose, I stretched my whole body up, straining to hear and see my beloved. Borne over the shining surface of a wave, the refrain was thrown to me, echoing from the wall of the high cliff above:

. . . my heart to the sea and the folk of the sea!

Then I saw Shian. She was sitting in the sun, on one of the pebble terraces, and in her arms was, surely, a strange white-looking object—Why, what was it?

Before I had time to study the scene the swell passed under me, and began to break soon after. Again I sank into the trough, but not before I had cried out aloud, in a voice cracked with excitement:

"Shian! Shian! Shian!"

What had she in her arms? A calf—seal in its first white coat? Or a human child? One or the other . . . It could be nothing else! I held myself ready to surf-ride the next swell, hoping it would break at the right moment to carry me to the shore. It reared up behind me, its shadow growing dark green and veined, taller than the last—for now I was nearer the beach.

Shian had heard me. I saw her bronze-yellow body standing erect beside the little white bundle which she had laid on the pebbles. I flung up my arms and shouted thrice again.

She did not reply. I saw her look down as if protectively upon the white object, perhaps with an irresolute gesture, for her bent head was quickly raised, and I saw her shade her eyes with one arm as she stared toward me. Then, as she turned her back, the swell broke over me. In my excitement I had forgotten to check my body to the surf-riding position, and for several seconds I was tumbled ignominiously upside down, my laugh of joy at finding Shian choked with a mouthful of salt water as the swell played with me—as with a corpse.

Gasping my way to the surface, I waited for the next surf-wave to catch up with me. Then I threw myself wildly forward, my limbs trimmed in the correct position. I felt a towering wall of green-blue embrace and swiftly lift me, gloriously, up and up until I sat in the ermine throne of its crest; and was borne luxuriously to the shore.

The wave flung me with a roar upon the high tide-terrace which for the moment hid the landward view. I stumbled over the familiar pebbles, waving my arms to maintain balance—and to receive Shian.

She had vanished, in those few blind moments—and the little white object with her. The black maw of the cave seemed to have swallowed both.

Was I suffering delusions—the hallucination which seemed to be my fate every time I returned to Kilcalla? I stood quite still, staring unbelievingly, fifty yards from the entrance to the cave.

In the silence of the spent wave I was sure I heard the cry of a human child. But of course young seals have a wail that is almost human. Could it be that Shian was caring for some orphan seal which, if so, must have been dropped prematurely? Or that a mother seal lay in the back of the cave, and Shian had returned the calf to her, before coming to meet me? Or could it be that Shian herself . . . ?

As if in answer to my wondering and longing, I saw her re-appear in the mouth of the cave. She was perfectly naked, with long hair flowing to her waist. For one second she looked at me, and I at her, one second of reassurance, then we ran together, my beautiful Shian and I, and enfolded each other in our ecstasy.

How shall I describe the happiness of the next hour? Words indeed were little used between us—with her lips tight pressed on mine. Once more her whole being was perfect, ripe and eager for my love; and my starved mind and hungry body quite flowed into hers. We remained united until the first tumultuous passion was satisfied. We had come together, this time as man and wife, with all the desire which our youth and love had built up in so long a separation. And once more Shian sought for and received me wholly, with a natural ease and abandon that I was to remember as the sweetest hour of my return.

There in the nest in the pebbles made by the striving of our bodies, in the warmth of the noon sun, we relaxed, talking at last ... freely, on my part for the first time.

Gradually Shian grew sleepy—a dear familiar habit I remembered of last year's matings. She held me prisoner in her arms as if even in sleep she would not let me go. I rested, remaining wakeful because I was far too happy and excited to let my thoughts fade into dreams.

Chapter Twelve

Shian was unchanged, a sea-woman still, but it seemed to me she had reached a new perfection physically. As she slept I examined her with loving interest. A thick down of sun-blond hair covered her body, but it was almost transparent, a natural protection for her fine sea-burned skin. The lines and curves remained shapely in their femaleness, the long legs firm and full of grace and strength below the rounded thighs. Shian had always had perfectly shaped legs, but her arms were unusually short and small. I stroked the arm that lay lovingly about my waist while she yet slept, and examined the little hand.

The webs were strong and well spread between the fingers, reaching almost to the last joint. Her nails were long and turned over to a sharp, almost claw-like point—this was a new development and made me uneasy. Shian had become more than ever a seal-woman. But I wanted nothing to mar our happiness this day. I kissed gently the sun-bleached skin, in my heart forgiving her all.

She stirred, smiling as she opened her fine dark eyes, then drew herself closer to me and fell to sleep again. Her full breasts were warmly against me, and now I saw that the nipples were rosy and much enlarged.

All winter—I had wondered, about this possibility . . . it was, after all, perfectly natural that she should become a mother. But I had expected in that case she would have sent me news. But no, after all, she neither had nor wished contact with civilization . . .

Of course . . . Shian was a mother! It was her own child—our child—that she had hidden in the cave! But why had she not shown it to me! In those days at the Holm of the Seals, then, Shian had already become pregnant, without my knowledge, and possibly without hers? No wonder she had not sought my embrace—a woman (or a seal), they said, sought not a mate at such times, even grew weary of his constant presence.

But now my curiosity was growing. I longed to have a glimpse of my child and to know it for son or daughter. Shian still slept, her arms firmly about me and I saw it would not be easy to slip away without waking her. It was almost as if she was afraid to lose me.

But see the child I must, and since she had not mentioned it to me I was the more anxious. Now I began to fear that it might be strange, a changeling child—had not our union been a strange, almost an unhuman one?

Cautiously I rolled over, as if seeking a new position in my sleep. Shian half-awoke, murmured a sweet word, and clutched me afresh. Gently I turned her over until her back was to me, and curled my body about hers, folding her arms in her lap, with my left arm shielding her. Thus had we often slept together in the first days at the Holm.

In this position her arms no longer held me, and I could slowly ease my body from hers, as she relaxed, and seemed gradually to fall into a deep sleep.

Yet when I was at last able to stand up and look down upon her exquisite form, with its new and exciting evidence of motherhood, I saw that her sleep had grown uneasy. How beautiful she was! I crept up the beach, stepping cautiously backward, reluctant to take my eyes from her darling form, afraid she might awake at any moment. Then my clumsy feet disturbed a peeble, and, though the sound was scarcely audible, Shian awoke instantly, sat up and gazed at me swiftly. I saw surprise in her face change to fear, and then fear vanish in a guarded smile.

"Have I slept long, Sea-wind?" she asked, smoothing back her sun-bleached hair over the downy shoulders.

I shook my head as I knelt down and kissed her warm lips.

"Not longer than I have—much." I laughed.

"Wonderful to hear you speak so well," she sighed, stretching her body luxuriously. "I knew the spell would be lifted when you had completed the long voyage."

We had scarcely discussed the restoration of speech to me, though Shian had accepted it with natural ease soon after we had embraced, and said a few—almost casual—words of joy for it. Now, in calmer mood she called me to sit down and talk of it, and of how the spell was broken.

As we talked I saw that she was thinking of something else. There were little lines on her forehead as the inward struggle went on. Was she trying to make up her mind to tell me of the child?

I could bear it no longer. I took her firmly in my arms; then challenged her with a laugh:

"Why won't you tell me the truth, Shian?"

"What?" she said, feigning an innocence she could not be feeling.

I touched her full breasts and pinched the nipples gently. She shrank back, as the milk spurted. A wild look was in her eyes.

"Am I not to see my own child?" I demanded, smiling, but my heart beat quickly with the beginnings of resentment that she should be so secretive.

She looked at me piercingly, then warm color suffused her brown cheeks and spread over her neck. Her eyes were cast down for a while. At last she said slowly: "You, prince of the sea, cannot have much interest in your sea—calf—when it is new-born? The male seals never go near the children . . ."

"Shian!" I cried.

I took her hand and pulled her toward the cave. She resisted at first, then suddenly, as if she would throw away all fears, she laughed and raced ahead of me. When I got to the cave I found her crouching over a white object lying in a nest of dried seaweed and grass.

"There's your little *mor-lo*!"

Shian spoke tenderly, proudly, but a little confused,

as if fearful of my reaction. She was still rosy with blushes, as if ashamed of being a mother.

Mor-lo! A Celtic name meaning sea-child, and one I had once heard Brendan call his sea-mad sister.

Chapter Thirteen

Fairer child than Mor-lo there was none; and in my eyes none more perfectly formed. Now I knew the tender joys of fatherhood joined with the raptures of a husband. Gradually Shian's seal-women fears left her as she saw how fondly I watched and played with our daughter.

Marvelous indeed was Mor-lo in several respects; for she was the most precious baby I had set eyes upon. Although only a few weeks old she was full of intelligence and activity. I was amazed to find that Shian would let her play in the deep rock pools, and more astonished to note that the child could already swim, and even make small dives.

Mor-lo loved the water. Her sweet round face would wrinkle with laughter as she sported in a sunlit sapphire of the pools. Swimming came to her naturally. I saw that she moved, without a conscious effort, by a seal-like undulation of her body and long legs. Sometimes her arms would be folded close to her body, **when she made a swift darting movement. But when** she floated, her little limbs were spread and the tiny fingers and toes were parted and clear of any webbing . . . well, almost . . . as yet.

Mor-lo was a human child—my child. Of that I was certain; and I was content. There was much of Shian in her face but even more of me—Mor-lo had my blue eyes and fair hair. Her skin, at first delicate and white, was getting rosier and brown in contact with the sea, the wind and the sun. Her short hair clung close to her little round head with tight curls, paler than ripening flax and with a green-golden tinge. She grew with great rapidity. Daily she appeared to be larger, less babyish and more understanding of her surroundings. Human she was, and yet no human child ever developed so rapidly.

In those late summer days our life at the caves was perfect. Shian was serene, fulfilled as a woman, and had quite forgotten that first misunderstanding or apprehension for her child. She sang each morning as at sunrise we took our bath in the surf. Then, while I caught our breakfast of small dainty fishes, she went to the pile of dried wrack and grasses at the back of the cave where we had slept so warmly beside our Mor-lo, and suckled the child.

Mor-lo, full-fed, would sleep for an hour afterwards, while we ate our whiting, mackerel, or green and ruby-scaled wrasse. The rest of the morning was given to play with Mor-lo.

It was at this play, as I watched, that I understood why Mor-lo was so expert in the water. Shian spent hours encouraging the child to learn the ways of the sea-folk. She would dive deep with Mor-lo clinging to her back, then she would gently release the child under water, and let her swim to the surface. Mor-lo was an apt pupil. Like a puppy she would retrieve a piece of cork or a stick thrown onto the shining mirror of a pool; and soon she learned to dive after a flat pebble, and catch it before it had quite see-sawed to the bottom.

It was plain to me that Shian would have Mor-lo become an independent sea-child as soon as she might—and Mor-lo learned with a speed that at times frightened me.

Beautiful Mor-lo! When the sun stood in the topaz zenith you would be hungry again. Then Shian fed you, and lulled you to sleep. Afterwards it was my turn—to talk and play with Shian. Until drowsiness and the noonday heat overcame us, and we would bask like the seals, for a while asleep, in the cool of the cliff shadows if the sun were too strong, or upon the edge of the sea when the Atlantic winds were blowing.

Thus refreshed I would rouse myself first, and stare

in wonder at my Shian's sleeping beauty. Those firm gracious limbs and the perfect body, those long curved eyelashes touching warm brown cheeks, the shining dark hair upon the sleek neck and shoulders. The curving breasts, rich with promise and fulfillment. The careless attitude of graceful repose upon the hard shingle and sand. O Shian!

Then I would comb her hair with my fingers, and stroke her downy body from the tight muscles of the shoulders to the rounded strength of the breast and belly, buttocks and thighs. And gradually Shian would awake, and turn to me, her body quivering and responsive.

We rolled and gamboled with the waves on the edge of the sea, for, like the love of the seals, it was here that Shian's passion grew stronger, with the silken water caressing our bodies.

By the sixth week Mor-lo was eating fish. Her first teeth had developed early, I knew, but I had not expected her to take solid food for several months. When I found Mor-lo eating from a shell full of sprats which I had brought to Shian, I took the food away from her. To my surprise Shian laughed and told me to let her eat as much as she liked.

Shian's hands went to her breasts.

"The child is hungry, Sea-wind. And my milk is slower . . ."

She touched the nipples gently, and I realized that they were grown redder than before. Shian smiled ruefully:

"Mor-lo has sharp teeth now!"

A few weeks later Mor-lo was completely weaned. Not only had her teeth become too sharp for her mother's breasts, but Shian's milk had quite ceased to flow. This Shian seemed to regard as perfectly natural. The cow seal suckles its calf at most four weeks. Shian had given milk to Mor-lo for eight only, and in the eighth week the child had subsisted largely on the soft pieces of raw fish, which I had endeavored to clean of bones, fearing they would choke her. But here again to my surprise Shian seemed almost indifferent about Mor-lo's food.

"Let her eat what she likes—she knows what she wants, now she is growing independent."

And Mor-lo did know what she wanted. She loved the tiny sprats and sand-eels which she herself caught in the rock pools. She would hunt for shrimps and prawns, which she ate after pinching off the tail and frontal carapace. I would help her, and sometimes Shian would join us when we sought the largest and ripest blue mussels clinging to the boulders at low tide. We hunted for the biggest whelk-shells, containing the juicy hermit-crabs. But usually Shian rested in the sunlight, content to watch us. Her body, which had grown slender during the nursing of our daughter, increased in weight, and eagerly, frequently, she sought the warmth, and satisfaction, of mine.

She was pleased when I suggested we ought to take Mor-lo north to the Yellow Strand to look for cockles in the fine sand. But when I said that Mor-lo must be taught to walk instead of wriggling seal-like on her belly over the pebbles, she did not answer. Once or twice, when I had made Mor-lo stand for a moment, holding her upright with my hands, I saw a frown on Shian's face.

It was the beginning of the struggle to direct the education of our child. For in my heart I knew I would not let Mor-lo become one of the sea-folk. It was all very well for Shian, born to such a life, to think that nothing but the sea mattered. But deep within me I knew I could not face a future of continuous exposure to the wildness of the ocean. Since the coming of Mor-lo there had been a gradual reaction. My longing for the land was slowly reasserting itself. It was borne upon me that now I had a new reason for returning to civilization—to educate my daughter and bring her up in the way a human child should go. Yet how to explain this without upsetting Shian I did not know. How explain to her that I wanted to see Mor-lo safe in pleasant clothes, learning to read and write, going to school with girls of her own age—that I wanted to be proud of Mor-lo before other humans? Shian, I knew, would think only of Mor-lo living the wild life of the seals, eating fish, going naked, facing the salt storms, growing up as a complete savage—ah, no, the thought of what Mor-lo would have to face if she became a sea-woman hurt me—even began to haunt me. One day soon I would have to insist that Shian come back with Mor-lo to my home.

A deep fear was growing in me as I thought of the long cold gales of winter.

These thoughts came to disturb my happiness—for I saw that Mor-lo continued to develop with astonishing rapidity; and her brain seemed to be keeping pace with her body. She knew me as a great friend and would watch my antics to please her with a humorous look on her cherubic face. More and more she played with me, since her mother left her alone so much; and I was only too willing to enjoy her attentions.

One morning a bitter wind blew from the southwest, with gray slanting rain. Shian lay at the mouth of the cave, resting, thoughtful and silent. It had been so cold and windy that I had kept Mor-lo under shelter, in spite of Shian's request that Mor-lo be allowed to go down to the rock pools for her usual exercise and play. Perhaps it was this little disagreement between us that made Shian thoughtful. And now, as the rain persisted and it was becoming obvious to me that Shian was right and I could not let our lively daughter remain a **prisoner in the cave all day, I felt unreasonably irritated.**

(But this was only the spark to inflame a new—yet familiar—resentment in my heart, which I had found difficult to fight down. While my ardor never changed, Shian's desire to possess me had gradually cooled; exactly as it had done a year ago at the Holm. She spent most of these latter days sleeping in the sun; as it seemed to me ignoring mate and child.)

Tired of playing with the speckled cave pebbles Mor-lo wriggled into the open. With a naughty challenging glance at me, she slithered down to her favorite pool. Neither Shian nor I followed. When we were alone I said firmly:

"Winter is near—it's time we took Mor-lo back with us, and made a human child of her, in a human home."

Shian remained silent, looking out to sea, her head turned from me. But I was determined to have my decision agreed to.

"Do you hear me, Shian?"

When she looked up I saw the reproach in her eyes. Soon tears began to fall—but I would not be so easily moved now. Like the seals, Shian cried very freely, sometimes at quite small things, and sometimes with joy. (In the seals there is no duct between eye and nostrils as in humans, so tears must flow outwardly whenever whenever they are emotionally moved: their oily tears help to lubricate and protect their large eyes against salt water.) My heart was softened, and I took her into my arms.

"Shian, please understand . . ."

She nodded, and put up her face to mine.

"We must not allow Mor-lo to become a wild beast," I pleaded, kissing the tears away. "What will become of her when she grows up and we are too old? For the sea will wear us both out, with its wild storms and cold gales. Even you were brought up to live the human way, with a warm house, clothes, books . . ."

"But it's so beautiful here . . . so clean and free!" Shian replied with a sudden smile. "Haven't we been perfectly happy here? No, don't ask me, Sea-wind, for I shall stay . . . and look how perfectly Mor-lo understands the sea already!"

"But we are *not* sea-men and -women, really, Shian. Look at our legs and arms. We have speech and reason, but the seals have only animal instinct," I protested, gently combing her long hair, sticky with salt.

"No, I find the seals far more intelligent than most humans I have met," she went on, still assuming an air of gaiety—or irresponsibility. "You have called me your princess; and you are truly a prince of the sea. Didn't you deal justice to the old bull who sought to be a tyrant over our people, the seals? They know you as their leader. O Sea-wind, they need you, you must go on leading them—always. Look how the race of land-bound humans is spoiling Kilcalla!" She waved her hand toward the cliff. "Soon perhaps you will have to lead the seal-herd safely to new calving grounds . . ."

"I can protect the seals from man better by living on the land," I retorted, "if only you would come back with me and claim your inheritance—the Kilcalla estate is yours by right of entail."

"But the people of the land suppose that I am dead," said Shian somberly. "No, I shall *never* go back there!"

She looked to the sea again. Away in the west a bright blue-green ellipse was spreading from the ocean horizon, rich and inviting as it drove the sullen veil of the rain-cloud toward the land.

"Look, dearest Sea-wind!"

She flung one arm about my waist—the contact made me shiver with delight. Her other arm pointed to the glorious light in the west.

"Besides," she added shyly a little later—as if a new thought had come to her, "besides, our children will be our bodyguard in our old age, our own strong sons and daughters—husband!"

Softly were these words whispered, while she quietly drew my hand in a natural movement against her breasts, down to her waist, to her smooth round belly, and looked into my eyes for understanding.

So! Like the seal-women, Shian had conceived again, so soon after weaning her first child? Like the cow seal, she now lost interest in the weaned one.

Of course I pretended to be pleased; but as I smiled at her and whispered my pleasure in her tiny ear, my mind already raced on, and fear and pride grew simultaneously. Great heaven, were we to raise a whole herd, a regiment of sea-children? And a son, could a son of mine be permitted to remain here and become a companion of the brainless lusty young bulls of the seal-herd? What was Shian thinking of!

Suddenly there was a wild screaming from Mor-lo.

Shian sprang forward, but I leaped to my feet and raced to the pool before her.

Poor Mor-lo had been gripped by a lobster as she played in the deep rock pool. The lobster hung on to her toes with his heavy pincer claw. Swiftly I grabbed Mor-lo and lifted her up. As her feet left the water the lobster let go and sank back to his crevice between the boulders—it was an immense old cock, dark blue. Mor-lo's foot was bleeding and she howled lustily.

I held the child, comforting her, while Shian gently sucked and licked the slight wound. But I was frightened and very angry now.

"You see," I said bitterly, "that's the sort of life we've got to give our children—to hunt and be hunted! Mor-lo shall go home with us tomorrow!"

Chapter Fourteen

No word was spoken after that. Shian seemed to be lost in deep thought. Only once did she turn and look at me, but there was no apparent recognition in her gaze, which seemed to pass right through me. At first I thought she was so upset as to wish deliberately to ignore me, while she calmed her thoughts; and, thinking so, I determined not to quarrel further with words; nor would I appear to weaken by resuming my pleading.

Mor-lo remained in my arms, warm against my naked chest. Without a glance at Shian, she soon fell asleep. In this way she comforted me, hardening my resolve to take her with me back to the land—perhaps tomorrow. In the night, I thought, I would coax Shian to join us. I would be a loving husband to her, but I would also be very firm. And while Mor-lo slept I reviewed the plans I had made already, for our future life. We would live somewhere deep in the country, perhaps where there was a clear river or a lake to swim in. For the present I had had enough of the sea. Besides, to live again by the salt shore would be too much of a temptation for my sea-mad Shian . . .

The sun had come out. When its warm yellow light woke Mor-lo, she began to play with my hair, and laugh and tease me. Soon, tired of this, she pulled my hand and drew me over to where Shian, lying flat like a seal upon the pebbles, elbows out and hands propping her brown cheeks, stared out to the shimmering line of the horizon. How lovable she looked in this attitude of pondering! But I would not give in—it was her turn this time. Too long had I striven to please her.

Mor-lo crawled upon her mother's back and pre-

123

tended to be riding a white sea-horse. It was a favorite game. But Shian ignored her completely.

I left them and went down to my usual fishing. I swam through the quivering emerald and speckled shallows into deeper water. As I hunted the plaice and the young flounders a new energy came to me: I was thinking of the quiet joys of an English home—of Shian, beautiful in evening dress, of Mor-lo asleep in a white cot; and of a fireside, old silver and thin slices of brown bread and butter, a pot of home-made jam! Yes, it was of these civilized delights I dreamed as the salt pricked my eyes, and my hands groped in the coarse grit of the ocean bed.

As I swam back to the beach, I saw that Mor-lo was alone, in the mouth of the cave. Shian was rolling by herself in the surf, scrubbing her body with sand. When I rode upon the pied arc of a wave, she saw me and turned away, deliberately ignoring me. At that my anger sprang violently into flame and as I shot past her, carried by the force of the flung wave, I attempted a thing I never dreamed I would dare to do, I reached out to seize her by the hair, brutally. Whether it was a bad aim on my part, or simply that Shian had seen my intention I do not know, but she slipped clear of me and dived. I was pitched forward, to land upright on my feet at the edge of the pebbles. I strode onwards, without a backward glance, until I had reached Mor-lo.

The child was pouting and tearful. She had been crying for some time. Had Shian been unkind to her? Why had not Shian taken her down as usual to play in the tide? I divined that her mother had forbidden her to leave the beach, either because of her sore foot, or, more likely, because she did not want Mor-lo to accompany her.

Wonder and dread in my heart, I cut open the fish and gave Mor-lo the fillets therefrom, while I frequently looked toward the breaking waves.

Shian came out of the sea, and now her body shone with the hard scouring she had given it. I saw her look up, as was her wont, to the high cliffs, watchful for surprise from the quarry-men who, working nearer to the edge now, might one day climb down and violate our fastness. Reassured by her glance, she did not seem to care to look further toward me, but turned to face the sea. She began combing her hair with her fingernails.

She remained by the sea's edge, sometimes sitting perfectly still, but occasionally she would move along the bank of pebbles and take up a new position. Always she gazed out to sea. Her restlessness grew as the sun went down. It was as if she was expecting something to happen. Or was she engaged in a mental struggle with the hard decision I had asked her to make? I believed it was so, and, therefore, although my heart was torn with anxiety and deepening desire to comfort her, I forced myself to remain upon the high beach, looking after Mor-lo. However I determined that Shian, whatever she decided, would have to obey me this time; and in the morning we would go up through the thickets to the cave in the escarpment we knew so well. There I would leave my wife and daughter while I went in search of clothes for them. This picture pleased me, but I could not banish my anxiety for Shian.

The sun vanished in a grayness that matched my increasing pity for Shian, whose form stood lonely against the velvet evening sea. A cold wind and a scudding mist had begun. Ah, it was hard for her to make such a sacrifice, and throw all her romantic plans to the four winds! But, mingled with my sadness—for I too in my heart, now that we were to leave the sea, had regrets—was the growing expectation of the happy civilized family life.

Mor-lo was sleepy. As Shian did not move I took the child to the nest within the cave, and rocked her in my arms until she began to breathe deeply. Then I laid her in the soft bed of dried grass, and stole out to find Shian.

Night had fallen. Lightly I ran to the foaming edge of a sea alight with phosphorescence, clamorous with the onshore prancing of little white horses. No sign of Shian, and no response to my calls.

I stifled the fear that rose within me. Nonsense!

Having so lately found each other, we could not part so easily, like this. She would be back soon, after she had enjoyed her farewell embrace of the sea? I would hold her in my arms, comforting her, praising her courage in making so hard a decision. I returned to the cave, and arranged with care our own couch beside that of Mor-lo, spreading there new dried wrack, woodrush and foxglove leaves from my store in the rock shelf above.

I lay awake. Hour after hour there was no welcome sound upon the nearby pebbles, and no shape upon the dim-lit shore. Only the sea grew wilder as the tide rose and the storm from the west increased. It did but match the wild beating of my heart.

Long before dawn came softly over the height of the cliffs I stood by the sea, harsh fear and tender longing striving within my chilled body. An hour passed like a day.

The wind had eased with the ebbing of the tide, but the morning mist still lay blanketing the lower air and the sea's sullen surface.

As I waited, my voice too hoarse to call any longer, I perceived the wind quite fail for a few minutes. Then a warmer air struck the back of my head as the land breeze flowed down to the sea. It rolled the mist back in sudden gusts. When the sun appeared I saw the black head of my Shian as she swam toward me—in the fifth white breaker!

She was laughing as she waved one arm, her eyes gleaming with their familiar light. I waited no longer. In my excitement I leaped through the shallows, and swam out to meet her. She threw herself into my arms.

After one brief embrace, she broke free.

"Sea-wind," she laughed, "they're coming home!"

I could not understand for a moment, not until she leaped up on the snow-crest of the swell and flung an arm to the west.

"The whole herd is coming home—look!"

As we rose I glimpsed, afar off, many dark heads swimming in the striped dawn waves. So, the seals were returning to their breeding caves and beaches!

But feel pleased about it I could not. I was, in fact, annoyed, and my annoyance rapidly increased as I realized the bitter truth that Shian's excitement was centered not on seeing me again but on the return of the herd from the Holm of the Seals.

So pleased and lively was she! She leaped and danced in the freedom of the surf. She begged me to swim with the main herd to the assembly beach. For a moment she seemed to have forgotten Mor-lo. I pointed to the cave, dumb with amazement and resentment.

"Mor-lo? Yes, of course, but she is . . . After all, isn't she three months old—a great big calf now? Old enough to look after herself! You bring her with you," she added as she saw my look of astonishment. "I'll go on—in any case, we must leave our cave; you see, the seal woman will need it at any moment now."

"Shian!"

I caught hold of her again, and turned her face toward me. What I saw there terrified me. Her eyes were unusually large and dark. Like those of a drugged person, they seemed to blaze with a wild unnatural light. Her nostrils were dilating rapidly, her breast heaving and her whole body was trembling as I held her.

I tightened my hold.

"Shian!" I pleaded. "Do you know what you are doing, and saying? Do you know me—Sea-wind—your husband?"

"Of course, yes, yes!" she panted and began to struggle. "But don't you see, we belong to the sea—we are part of the great herd of the Western Ocean! We must go with them, and stay with them—always!"

Three great cow seals, thrush-striped coats distended with unborn calf, were swimming through the shallows, making for our beach. But the main body of the seals had turned to the south and were even now moving toward the Twelve Sisters caves. The last mist had gone and the sun was driving a late moon low over the darker western sea.

The more I tried to coax Shian the wilder grew her

struggles. Suddenly I desisted—almost roughly I released her, saying:

"If you care for the seal herd above your mate and child, why, then, go your way and I will go mine!"

Shian instantly dived.

She came up some distance away, but did not look back at first . . .

The last I saw of her she had mingled with the scores of bobbing seal heads, all making for the Twelve Sisters.

After I had come ashore I watched until the blue water and the black distance had quite devoured my sea-wife. Once only did she pause and turn and look back.

And then went on.

Chapter Fifteen

Of the difficulties and little pleasures, the fears and re-
awakening hopes, that accompanied our journey, the
journey of Mor-lo and myself, I need not write. There
was no one to challenge my return with a baby daughter. I had sent a telegram to my sister, asking her to
meet our train on arrival in London. I wanted her to
take care of Mor-lo while I returned to fetch Shian.
She was delighted to arrange a nursery for Mor-lo in
my small house, and see about her comfort with the ut-
most affection.

The wondering child was in the best possible
hands—and, thank heaven, away from the spell which
the sea had begun to put on her.

"She's exactly like you!" my sister said enthusiasti-
cally. "What is her mother like?"

"A very beautiful woman," I replied evasively, adding that all explanations would follow when I brought
my wife home—in a few weeks' time.

At first I had foolishly supposed I could abandon
Shian—let her live out one more winter in the wild life
she was so fitted for. We had parted in anger—at least
on my side; but now in cold blood I had come to realize that it had been a natural, if unhuman and seal-like,
emotion on her part. Like the female seal, now that she
had conceived again, she had become indifferent to her
weaned child, and had no immediate need of a mate. It
was a fact that for nine months of the seal's annual
cycle males and females lived virtually separate lives, a
divided herd.

Nevertheless Shian was human; and I had not been
home for a single day before I ardently desired to re-

turn and find her—before she became completely a savage again. Although in my heart I knew she would refuse to come (for in truth if I found civilization and the petty restraints of clothes and city conventions hard to accustom myself to, how much more difficult and impossible would they be for Shian?), I still believed it was my duty to reason with her. How could she abandon Mor-lo like this?

But I determined that I would never take Mor-lo back to Kilcalla.

As it happened I found my affairs in a thorough mess. I could not afford to return that winter to Ireland. My clever chief clerk had absconded with a large sum of money on the day after I re-appeared in the office.

Meanwhile my immediate joy was to watch my darling Mor-lo, now as devoted to my sister as she was to her father.

The months passed; winter vanished, and spring came, but still I delayed my return to collect Shian. I must be patient.

Making a rough calculation, I saw that Shian had carried Mor-lo for the normal human pregnancy of nine months (the gestation period of the Atlantic seal is one year, less two weeks). It comforted me that this was evidence of her human physiology, for at times I had felt that in truth she had been born of a seal mating. Now, since she had made it plain that she had conceived again, within a few months of Mor-lo's birth, I could estimate when our second child would be born. A thought which constantly filled me with hope as well as a great fear. A male child of mine perhaps ... out there, in the wild storms? Good God!

Kilcalla was a desolate scene when at last I arrived, about the estimated date for Shian's confinement, which I felt sure would be in the same place where Mor-lo had been born, close to the dark cave where, according to her grandparents, Shian herself had been born—or found.

The great forest was now much felled, the slate

quarry in full operation with mechanical chisels and machinery. I encountered Iolo Rees, the manager, who politely asked me my business. On my describing myself as an amateur naturalist, which was both the truth and my excuse for rambling along these cliffs and shores, he invited me to coffee in his office. A go-getter, but well educated, he claimed to be interested in nature himself. As the Welsh do, he talked rapidly, explaining that he had endeavored to save the remnant of deer that once roamed the estate, but the felling had been too much for them, and it was difficult to keep the men from poaching. Life was rather dull in this wild uninhabited country. They needed a bit of amusement. He was sorry about the deer, but feared they had all disappeared. As for the seals . . .

His men had asked if they might indulge in a bit of seal-shooting the other Sunday. The skins would be worth quite a bit. A local man thought he knew where they bred: down in the caves at the far end of the big strand. It had been quite an exciting expedition, with guns, clubs and torches. They had started very early last Sunday morning, and after sandwiches and a drink on top of the cliffs, while waiting for the tide to ebb, they had been shown by their guide down the old wreckers' path, very steep and much overgrown, to the caves where the seals bred. The thing to do was to take the seals by surprise.

When it came actually to entering the caves the courage of the local guide—an oldish man—had failed. This Irishman had suddenly withdrawn, muttering something fanciful about the place being haunted by the ghosts of the O'Malleys who once owned all this corner of Ireland.

They could hear seal moans inside the caves, so they had not been much alarmed or surprised that these human-like wails had given rise to the old fellow's superstitious talk. It was agreed that, as they were known to be savage and powerful animals, one man should go ahead into each cave and try to flush the seals out, and that the others would then club the beasts in the open as they shuffled down to the sea. If they escaped the clubs, then the men with the guns would be able to fire safely seawards and have a bit of sport trying to shoot them before they reached the water. Yes, said Iolo Rees, it had been carefully planned and timed. They had arrived at the first cave exactly at low water, which made it accessible and gave them plenty of time to tackle the seals while the tide was far out.

What had happened? I asked; and he seemed amused at my whispered words, mistaking, in the dim light of the dusty office, my look of horror for one of breathless interest.

Well, he went on, something very odd had happened in one of the deepest caves, and there was no way of accounting for it, rightly . . .

Young Ted—a keen hunter—had taken a torch and tiptoed quietly into this big cave, and vanished for several minutes. Then he had suddenly given a wild yell and rushed out again. He had shouted that there were dozens of monster seals lying there; but also something else—he swore he'd seen a seal with a human face and hair! In fact he insisted, later, that it was a genuine mermaid he had seen!

Close upon his heels had come a dozen frightened seals, lolloping along on their bellies, making for the sea. There hadn't been time to discuss the mermaid story. The men with the bully sticks had got to work and knocked down six big cows, and those with rifles had shot or wounded the rest. The edge of the sea had been red with blood from the *battue*.

Rees sighed. It had been an unholy bloody mess . . .

"Duw, man! I hadn't realized until it was too late, that all these seals were pregnant mothers. If only I had known beforehand! It was only when we began to skin and cut them up that I realized this."

He looked at me—the confessed nature-lover—apologetically; and added that, personally, he thought he would never shoot a seal again. Why, the big old seals, as they died, moaned horribly and wept real tears! They were very nearly human. The poor devils! He had called the expedition off after that. In any case, the tide was coming in rapidly, and they had enough to do skinning nine or ten great seals, each weighing a good quarter-ton!

The mermaid? Ah, yes, that had been a curious business, and he had never really got to the bottom of it. When young Ted, as they worked at skinning the seals, continued to insist upon having seen something in the cave that looked like a cross between a mermaid, a seal, and a witch, he, Iolo, had grown curious, and at last had decided, especially as the superstitious local man had said he had better not interfere with such things, and the tide was rising very quickly (but chiefly because no one else seemed to be anxious to enter the cave again), that he would nip in and investigate quickly.

He had taken a rifle and lashed a flashlight along the barrel, so that the beam of its light automatically and accurately sighted long the line of fire. With this at the ready he had cautiously entered the big cave. It was narrow at first, widening to a steep tide-washed pebble beach and again narrowing to a kind of low chamber at the back, quite in the darkness.

I nodded, my throat harsh and dry. He had described Shian's cave, where Mor-lo had been born.

"In the poor light of the torch I could see nothing at first except a new-born seal calf in long white fur," he continued, "and I decided, on spotting this, that Ted had imagined things about this object, which lay on the inner beach of pebbles. In fact, I chuckled at the thought of teasing Ted about it; I left it in peace—its discovery removed some of the creepiness of this dank cavern and the feeling of the supernatural which such places always give me. So I moved forward to finish my exploration in quite a cheerful spirit . . . Then, right at the end of the cave, wedged against the polished rock wall, under an overhanging rock, I saw another and larger animal moving slightly. Unfortunately, the torch battery was not a fresh one and the light was getting dimmer and dimmer. I must say that what I had seen, though, gave me a start, for I'll swear I saw a head with long hair, and I could almost swear I saw human arms, not seal flippers resting on the rock. I

133

couldn't see a face clearly, it was partly hidden by black hair. But I'll swear I had a glimpse of a woman-like form, with breasts and a distinct waist—quite naked; not as white as a young seal in its first coat, but still, paler than a grown seal is."

"What happened next?" I asked desperately, for Iolo Rees had stopped, with a sigh, and was finishing his coffee thoughtfully. At last he resumed:

"What happened next was a whole series of tanta-lizing and stupid accidents. I leaned forward to get a better view and cracked my head devilishly hard on the roof of the cave, which, in my excitement, I hadn't no-ticed came so low. As near as possible I pulled the trigger, but not quite, for I was terrified—just for one half-second—that some devil of the cave had struck me a blow! My finger slipped off the trigger and the rifle dropped, the tip of the barrel hitting the grit on the floor of the cave. This jarring caused the torch to go right out . . . Bloody hell!"

He paused and looked at me dramatically, evidently enjoying the suspense I was in. I signed to him to go on.

"There was absolute silence in the cave—it was so still that I could hear the sea far off at the entrance to the cave. All my superstitious fears came back to me as I stood there in the dark listening, and my heart pounding. Then a very low sigh seemed to come from well in front of me. At least, I *thought* I heard a sigh at the time, but now I can't be sure that it wasn't the faint echo of the breaking waves on the beach below. Anyway, you bet, I didn't stay listening any longer! I'd had enough! When I found the torch had given out, and knowing that my rifle barrel was blocked with grit, I suddenly felt mighty helpless—and in great danger. I'm not ashamed to admit I had a bad attack of claus-trophobia! I grabbed the gun and stumbled back toward the mouth of that horrible cave. I fell headlong several times, bruising myself badly on rocks here and there, and once over the spongy body of the young seal—and that didn't improve my nerves or temper!

Especially as the little beast growled at me, and nipped my leg with its needle teeth!

"The tide was splashing over the entrance to the cave and Ted was bawling to me to hurry up. As it was I got a thorough wetting in dodging out to the open beach. There was not a hope of getting back with fresh torches on that tide. Not that I was anxious to go back just then, I may as well admit!"

He poured more coffee into our cups. I tried to appear calm as I asked him if he had been back to the cave since?

"I have. And the very next day. Anyway we had to go down to finish cleaning up the seals, and bring sacks and ropes to haul up the spoils. Pretty heavy, those sealskins, thick with blubber, and those lumps of seal meat which the men wanted to cook—real red meat, you know, these beasts aren't fish. As for myself, I was definitely curious about the mysterious object in the back of that cave. You see, Ted continued to swear that he had seen the mermaid apparition in the middle of the cave, lying half upright *beside* a white calf, and it must have moved, because I had seen it right at the very end of the cave—as if it had been trying to hide from me. But now I feel—to be absolutely honest— rather confused about the whole experience; and sometimes I believe that I was mistaken about the human moan I heard. It could have been an echo from the sea, or the men, outside, or it could have been another baby seal up there beside the so-called mermaid, but hidden from me. After all it was probably only another cow with her calf, though it looked very human . . . in the half-dark."

He paused. Trying to hide my terrible fears, I asked:

"Yes? And what did you find when you went back next day?"

"Nothing. Nothing at all!"

"Nothing!" I said, unspeakably relieved. "Nothing at all?"

"Nothing at all—in any of the caves."

"Not even the young white calf?"

"Not even the white calf. All the caves were absolutely empty, though we explored every one we could reach, with new batteries in our torches. From end to end it looked as if the big tides had swept everything clean as a whistle."

"But you did not get into every cave, surely?"

"I think we did—all we could find to get into, anyway. I counted at least twelve fine caves altogether, large or not so large, which we managed to examine, but there wasn't a seal—bull, cow or calf—to be found."

"The whole herd had moved off?"

"Must have. We saw not a single thing, except three carcasses washed ashore—all cows evidently mortally wounded the day before. In fact one was just about alive, a huge old matron with opaque eyes—she must have been blind a long time, I would guess. Of course we put her out of her misery, poor old girl."

"But surely," I argued, trying to conceal my mingled relief and disgust, "the calf must have been somewhere—it was too young to go to the sea?"

"As for that," said Iolo, after some thought, "I'm not acquainted enough with the habits of seals to be able to say. All I know is that we never saw it again. But I tell you what, we'll go down and have another look, if you are interested, on the next suitable low tide. It's a magnificent place—the caves are worth exploring for their own sake. Perhaps the seals will be back again. Are you staying long in the district? Have another coffee?"

But I made excuses, saying I had to go back home almost at once; feeling I might do Iolo some physical harm if I got him alone in the caves, to pay him out for his so-called "sport." I wanted only to escape and hurry down alone to find Shian. If she had been in that cave, then it seemed she must be alive, and had escaped, perhaps with the calf she seemed to have been nursing—her calf? I mean, her child . . . my child . . . perhaps my son?"

Seeing my angry and bitter look, Iolo Rees said, "Mind you, I'd never shoot seals myself again, at this time of year, when they are full of pup, or nursing their babies. But it's not so easy to control the men. And there's a bounty on each seal killed, paid by the Fisheries Board . . ."

Choking with fear and hope I left the office unceremoniously, saying, "It's beastly—horrible! For God's sake, let them alone in future! At least while they're breeding!"

To throw him off my scent I walked eastwards inland along the track to the hamlet. As soon as I reached the cover of the first thicket, I began to run in a wide circle through the multiliated forest, working my way toward the strand and the caves.

There is little more for me to record here. I do not remember how many days—which seemed like years—I searched along the Kilcalla shore. But I found not my Shian, nor any sign of the great seal herd. Since the men were working closer to the cliff edge now, loosening the slate with dynamite each day, I made my searches chiefly at night, under a yellow harvest moon and a clear sky filled with stars. I hoped that the seals would return under cover of darkness.

It was very beautiful then, beside the restless silver-touched water, but my heart was filled only with a great loneliness. As each day and night passed in my vain search I began to think that Shian had indeed been dead, that her body had been washed out of the cave by the high tide, after the *battue*.

One midnight, as I swam in the shallows, I believed I heard the crying moan of a seal—a young seal, which has such a human wail. Or was it a fragment of the Song of the Sea? It seemed to come from the outer edge, the menhir rocks of the southern cape. Eagerly, furiously, I swam along the edge of the slate beach, calling out a name until I was hoarse. I waded ashore and ran along the pebbles to reach the cape more swiftly. Then I dived into the water and swam the last few hundred yards to reach the great rocks which had seemed to reflect the solitary cry. Or was it merely the echo of my own weary call?

Upon the high terrace I found the wet trail of some

large sea-animal, a long wide smear shining upon the rock in the moonlight. It must have been made by a slender body, perhaps that of a young or yearling seal? Or was it the mark of Lutra the otter, who in late summer was apt to leave the fresh water to hunt the conger eels among the rocks at low tide? But otters whistle—they do not moan.

The cold wind swept toward me, singing a faint mocking song in the great tumbled menhirs above me. I listened intently, and shivered, the cooling sweat of my haste pricking my back like ice. This song was only the moan of the sea-wind in the pitiless rocks. I called out again, shivering more violently. At night the sea is warm; I threw myself down as a foaming wave rose up to meet me.

Suddenly I knew I must swim to the Holm of the Seals.

I had not swum more than half a mile before cramp gripped my legs. Slowly releasing the agony by stretching them, I grew inexpressibly weary. I was mentally and physically exhausted. The sea air seemed to penetrate my skin with Arctic coldness when I floated at the surface. There was no doubt I could stand less of exposure now. I should never reach the Holm—except by boat. In my despair and bitterness I felt angry with Shian once more. It was she who had deserted me—Shian, mermaid, sea-woman, nay—witch of the sea!

I swam back, slowly, reluctantly, feebly. I was half drowned by the time I flung myself to rest on the pebbles.

Days later, when the sea was calm for a week, I hired a powerful motor boat, and searched the whole of the shore north and south of the Kilcalla Strand. I spent a whole day at the Lemon Reef, and Great and Little Skellig Rocks. I saw only a few seals—at a distance; they were quite wild and unapproachable.

I climbed ashore and explored every inch of the Holm. It was deserted: all the sea-birds had flown, and not a single seal appeared. The long grass of summer

138

was gale-withered and brown. If Shian had been there I should have noted at least the slight track she would have made up to the remains of the hut I had built for her. But there was no sign of human occupation.

Even the Lemon Reef was empty. On our return, as we passed by, the tide was low, and the sea dead calm. The seals should have been there, basking.

But there was nothing.

Nothing at all.

Epilogue

Of course I do not expect people to believe this account of my adventures with my seal-woman. This record is principally for my own reading; but I have left it to be opened by Mor-lo after my death. Let her believe what she will about her mother. At the time I write this she is too young to be told the truth.

Upon my sister I failed to make any impressions when in an inspired but unguarded moment I cautiously began to take her into my confidence. But seeing her amused, tolerant incredulity I stopped short. She was perfectly happy ministering unreservedly to Mor-lo's wants (I fear we shall spoil the child between us). My sister has never said so, but I sensed that she believed I had spent those several holidays in Ireland in a certain abandoned fashion, and that what had happened to Mor-lo's mother was too delicate a question to probe deeply. Clearly she believed that Mor-lo was my love-child; but loyally she told our curious friends that I had lost my wife soon after the birth of my daughter. Truly I had lost Shian . . .

Mor-lo has astonishing health and vitality. She loves to hear me tell simple tales of the folk of the sea, and of the watery kingdom in the west where they dwell. For strangely, like her great-grandparents O'Malley, I have found a new pleasure, a form of consolation, in repeating to her the tales told by the wind in the treetops, and by the storms of the sea, exactly as her mother had recited them to me. I am sure that Mor-lo, taken away from the sea at three months of age, does not really remember Kilcalla; and I read only a naïve childish curiosity when she asks when I am going to show her the haunts of the leprechauns, the mermaids and the seals.

Of course I have no intention of taking Mor-lo back to her birthplace, even though Kilcalla is still hers—did the Public Trustee but know it. Not only would I fail to establish her right to it, but I fear that if she went there, she would be quite disappointed. It is no longer the refuge of the wild things. The forest is now almost entirely stripped and, although the slate quarries are nearly exhausted, the Public Trustee had maintained some employment by establishing new farms and cottages on the estate.

The last deer has been killed, or fled. At the moment a small but thriving human population has taken the place of the wild one. The O'Malley private chapel has been rebuilt and enlarged into a public church with a resident priest. The old tablets to long-dead O'Malleys are rubbed bright, and their memorable association with the princedoms of the past mentioned in a little booklet, written by a local historian which is on sale there. The inn has a new landlord and a busier clientele, including summer tourists.

Only the pebble shore and, above it, the sheer cliff and the almost inaccessible escarpment remain unchanged, the haunt yet of badger, fox and sea-bird. Below it, but at rare intervals, a few seals gather and fish in the white run of the currents; but as man continues to hunt them—and there is now a small bounty for each snout, paid by the local fishery interests—they are quite wild and difficult to watch. Perhaps they have not forgotten the great slaughter of pregnant cows? At any rate they no longer lie out on the strand, or visit the caves of Kilcalla, even by night.

How do I know this? There were some days in the late summers and autumns of the last few years when I found the air of town and home quite insufferable. The ineradicable heartache grew too strong to resist any longer. Making some excuse of seeing my agents in the country, I have left Mor-lo in the care of my sister, and made secret lone journeys to the west.

That is how I know.

SONG OF THE SEAL-WOMAN
(a translation)

The refrain:
Song of my heart, O Sea, thou art singing,
Down there in the great strand thou are beating,
Thy music is in my ear when of thee I am dreaming,
For I have given my heart to the sea
  and the folk of the sea.

The verses (sung at random, that is in no particular or-
der, and freely altered):
Song of my heart, O Sea, thou art singing:
Down there on the gray reefs the seals are moaning,
My feet are flying to the tide, to the seaweed,
I stand on the shore with the cool waves
  foaming over my toes,
For I have given my heart to the sea
  and the folk of the sea.

Song of my heart, O Sea, thou art singing:
Down there in the sunlight the seals are basking,
The old ones on the high rocks, the young ones below,
Where the tide flows they will leave their rock couches,
For I have given my heart to the sea
  and the folk of the sea.

Song of my heart, O Sea, thou art singing:
In the wild bay the seals are diving for fishes,
The young calves are playing in the warmth
  of the shallows
As the tide creeps slowly over the sun-blessed strand;

For I have given my heart to the sea
and the folk of the sea.

Song of my heart, O Sea, thou art singing:
The sea-birds are flying from the rising waves,
The sea folk are flocking to the cool granite caves,
And I am calling to the brown heads
swimming by my feet;
For I have given my heart to the sea
and the folk of the sea.

Song of my heart, O Sea, thou art singing:
My heart's love he is prince over the seals;
I shall climb down each day to the soft sandy beaches,
To the shadows of the long caves in the granite cliffs;
For I have given my heart to the sea
and the folk of the sea.

Song of my heart, O Sea, thou art singing:
There in the red cave dwells the old cow seal,
Never stirring until her white calf can swim
And I am singing and stroking the gray woman
and her fine child;
For I have given my heart to the sea
and the folk of the sea.

Song of my heart, O Sea, thou art singing:
Soon the speckled calves and their mothers are moving,
Are swimming the long channel to the sun and the ocean,
They are leaving me lonely by the edge of the shore;
For I have given my heart to the sea
and the folk of the sea.

Song of my heart, O Sea, thou art singing:
In the spring he will come—my prince from the ocean.
I have waited him long since the turn of the year;
He will show me the way to the sunlit Holm of the Seals;
For I have given my heart to the sea
and the folk of the sea.

Song of my heart, O Sea, thou art singing:
We shall follow the seals on the wings of the waves,
My prince and I shall ride the saddles of white horses,
He will crown me his queen in the far Holm of the Seals,
For I have given my heart to the sea
*   and the folk of the sea.*